DRAGON KIN

JAE & FENDELLEN

SHAE GEARY

AUDREY FAYE

FIREWEED PUBLISHING

COPYRIGHT

PROLOGUE

*P*eace. *It was a thing that had not been celebrated in her lifetime, and Lovissa did not yet trust that it would stay, but the fires of midwinter burned and her dragons rejoiced, not caring what the spring might bring. They had not lost a single dragon since midsummer, and for those used to living battle to battle, it was a heady feeling indeed.*

She looked over at the fierce black dragon who had landed silently at her side as the sun set and been a lurking shadow ever since. Watching the fires, but not joining them. ::You worry that they will be weaker when it is time to fight again.::

::Perhaps.:: Baraken sounded thoughtful. ::Or perhaps they gain in strength and purpose. There are many who pair up. We will have new hatchlings when the sun warms the skies again.::

They always had one or two, but she knew what he meant. Peace, even a most tenuous one, came with hope. ::Marphus reports that the snow levels on the south slopes are low. The coming year will not be any easier for those elf clans.:: Drought had weakened the elves—and kept her dragons alive.

::The north is more worrisome.::

She looked over at the warrior who had delivered many of their peace offerings. *::They have not ignored our gifts.::* Some on the southern slopes had died rather than accept food from a dragon.

Some—but not all.

Baraken's eyes did not leave the fires.

She did not need his words to be spoken. She knew he hated every morsel of food and every drop of water delivered to their enemies. But he said nothing even as he returned with empty claws. There was nothing to say. The clans of the north accepted their gifts, but they had not yet agreed to a cease fire.

Lovissa knew her dragons doubted, and in the quiet of her own cave, she doubted with them. But they must not see their queen waver. *::If it is war they want in the spring, they shall have it.::* Adding a little meat to their weak bones would not change the battles overmuch—and perhaps they, too, breathed in the air of a crisp midwinter in which no elves had died and let themselves dream of peace.

Or perhaps she was weak, ensnared by visions of a future in which elves were no longer the enemy.

Baraken's head turned a fraction. *::I did not know you doubted.::*

Lovissa sighed. She would not have burdened him with her own uncertainty. *::The ashes spoke most clearly.::*

::Indeed.:: A long pause. *::And we have not been murdered in our caves as we slept.::*

There were far too many guards posted for such a thing, but again, she heard what he did not say. Even her finest warrior dared to hope. *::Perhaps, in the spring, they will be willing to talk* *of peace.:: Even one or two clans of the north would be a boon. Their dragonkiller arrows flew more swiftly than those of the southern slopes.*

There was a disturbance in the valley below. She could feel it —a shifting of attention away from the fires and into the dark.

Baraken snapped to attention beside her.

A path opened to the central fire, and then she heard the flapping, felt the disturbed air of a dragon coming in fast and hard.

Her heart leaped as a small, lithe body landed with an abruptness that would embarrass him later. Timot. He was one who guarded the outer edges of the valley, overflying the northern slopes. Surely the elves did not come now. The snow had blocked the passes two moons past.

She spread her wings. Her landing would be no better than his, but he clearly came with news, and she would hear it first. She felt Baraken take to the air behind her, far more gracefully.

She set her feet down in front of Timot, her head held high. "You have news?"

He gulped. "Four elves. Where the Marash is highest."

The lowest of the passes, and the only one reachable in the inhospitable weather of midwinter. "Are they armed?" Four elves were no threat, but perhaps more had found a way to hide themselves in the snow.

Timot shook his head slowly. "They bade me to land."

Every dragon within earshot hissed.

He quivered, and she could see the doubt in his eyes.

She had been a scout once. They were chosen as much for their good judgment as their flying skills. She nodded. She would hear the rest of his story.

He gulped. "They put down their weapons and waved. They

did not appear to be a threat, and I thought I recognized two of them from the hunting parties."

Timot often flew scouting trips, and against her better judgment, he had let himself be seen. He had also delivered many of their gifts. "So you landed." A foolhardy and brave act, but he had proven himself to be the second many times over, and rarely the first.

Timot looked as if he wished to hide behind the nearest rock, but he held the gaze of his queen. "I did. They kept their hands high, and two stayed far back."

The ones who would avenge the other two should the dragon attack. Lovissa swallowed. He had been a brave and foolish dragon indeed.

"They put a bowl. On the ground." Timot's throat clicked. A dragon's remembered terror. "It smelled of meat, and other things I did not recognize."

Lovissa's entire body stiffened. "They brought you a gift? Of food?"

Something in Timot's gaze eased. "I did not know if it was a gift or poison. But I did not want to start a battle by believing it to be poison." He swallowed, and his throat clicked again. "I took only a very small taste at first."

Just as they taught the hatchlings to do with an unfamiliar berry. Lovissa held her breath, just like every other dragon within earshot. Waiting to hear the rest of Timor's story.

His breath huffed out in smoke and remembered fear—and something else. "It was good. It tasted of meat and berries."

It clearly hadn't killed him, so they would speak of slow-acting poisons later. "Tell me of the elves, Timot."

She could see his confusion. "I didn't understand their words, and they do strange things with their faces and their arms. But *when I finished the bowl, the smallest one brought me this." He held out his claws.*

Lovissa felt alarm billow through the valley—and then awe.

A dragonkiller arrow.

Broken in two.

PART I
MIDWINTER'S NIGHT

CHAPTER 1

It was the kind of cold Gran called crackling, where the air froze as soon as you breathed it out, like winter was trying to take your soul and turn it to ice. Or at least that's what the villagers thought, huddled around their hearths on this, the longest night of the year. They would be asleep by now, bedrolls pulled close to the fire, or deep enough in their cups to take little notice of strange things in the night.

Here in the high mountains, the villagers knew better than to notice strange.

Jae slid out of her cloak, shivering a little, even though she didn't feel the cold like the others. It still slapped against her skin, a crisp wind with no manners. She tipped her head back as it snatched at her hair, streaming it out behind her. She loved the wind currents of her mountains, unlike the other villagers, who complained bitterly. Gran said it was because she'd been born on the rocks.

Left out on the mountain to die, the others said, but

they never did it where Gran could hear. Those who had when Jae was younger found themselves on the wrong end of a healer's wrath the next time they got sick.

Gran never refused to heal anyone, but her brews could be made to damn near kill you before they healed you. Young Mellie's brews tasted better, but they didn't always work as well, so the village had learned to be kind to Jae, even if she was a foundling and mountain strange right down to her bones.

Jae worked quickly, unwrapping the wide band of cloth from around her middle. She shivered anew as the cold blew right threw her thick woolen dress, and then her wings snapped free and she didn't care about the weather anymore. She took one more furtive look around for anyone wandering drunk too far from their bed. In summer, she went farther from the village before she took to the skies, but in winter, Gran worried if she strayed too far.

A balance, always. Gran and her own growing healer skills kept her safe, so long as she didn't allow the villagers to look overlong at her differences. They'd grown used to her heavy cloaks, even when summer came to the high mountains. And only Mellie and Gran knew she took to the skies at night.

She had to. The sky had always called to her. In the daytime, too, but Gran's eyes had always looked pinched and afraid when little Jae had forgotten and flapped herself toward the sun, so bigger Jae had learned to keep her feet on the ground and her wings safely bound up under her cloak while the sun was out.

She folded her cloak and binding cloth, leaving them in

a neat pile by a tree with gnarled branches that were easy to see, even from the darkest night sky. Then she unfurled her wings, sighing in gratitude as they stretched out for the first time in three days. They didn't cramp anymore since she'd stopped growing, but it still felt magnificent to reach them out as far as they could go, letting them flutter in the wind so her feathers all lined up properly. She stretched out her arms, too, and let the fierce mountain wind blow straight at her face.

The villagers might complain bitterly about that wind, but they'd never taken a ride on its magic. She laughed as a strong gust nearly lifted her feet off the ground, and then she let her wings move. Not flapping, really—with the wind this strong, it wasn't needed. She just let the gust catch her and lift her up, tossing her into the sky for no other reason than it wanted to play.

She swirled on her way up, dipping and diving and weaving as the six mountains that rose up around her village all split and tangled and teased the air under her wings. It was a wild ride, one that spoke of midwinter storms coming, the kind that would keep even hardy high-mountain villagers wrapped up tight in their huts.

But it wasn't storming yet. The skies were crisp and clear and full of stars. Jae reached up as if to cup them in her hands, and laughed as the air rushed through her fingers. Then she tucked her hands under her wings, deep in the warm feathers. She would spend as much of this night in the sky as she could, and she knew well what happened to villagers who let their fingers turn to ice. They were the one part of her that sometimes felt the cold, and she intended to be like Gran, who had managed to reach old age with all her fingers and all her teeth.

Jae felt her heart squeeze even as she reveled in the tumbling air of the night sky. The old woman who had raised her had talked once, deep in her cups, about touching the stars. She would love this, at least the parts that involved the beauty of the night sky. The rest was Jae's, and hers alone. Gran was a woman who kept both feet firmly on the ground, and generally her eyes there too, looking for the plants that ended up in her brews.

Which was how she had found a baby left on the side of the mountain.

And insisted, firmly, that even a baby with wings on her back had the right to live and breathe and grow up to be a productive part of the village.

It had worked, mostly.

Gran had held the stories of demons and magics and curses at bay, and when Jae had grown old enough to understand the whispers, she had wrapped cloth around her wings and done her best to be a healer's apprentice no different from Mellie.

Except for taking to the skies at night. That, she could not give up, even for safety. Jae tipped one of her wings toward the highest mountain, catching a draft rising up from the ground, slightly warmer than the deep winter chill of all the others. In summer, that wind would blow her right up over the peak, higher even than the mountain eagles that sometimes came to circle her in the night.

They never came too close. Wary, like all wild things.

And tame ones, too. The people of the village watched

her with those same eyes, even those she considered her friends.

Cautious acceptance—but they never forgot.

Jae sighed. Even with stars beyond counting to keep her company, loneliness followed her to the sky. The knowing, deep in her bones, that she would always be other. Tolerated, yes. Welcomed, even, especially when she brought brews made from ingredients found far from the village. But she would never have bashful boys bringing flowers to her door or a babe of her own in her arms or a family to gather around and listen to her stories as she grew old.

The loneliness had sharpened this winter, watching Mellie's belly swell with her second child.

Jae rolled over onto her back, coasting under a blanket of stars, her feathers chiding the winds trying to snatch her out of the sky. Gran would have no patience for her lonely talk. Life was about being useful, about fixing things before they broke, or after, if absolutely necessary. Gran had no patience for those who visited their cups overmuch, helped by a heavy dose of winter mead or not.

Jae let the wind tug her toward the ground and then swooped up again, laughing as her skirt blew around her ears. Entirely indecent, but there was no one in the skies to care.

She stretched her wings, riding the primary current down the valley toward the village. She hadn't wandered tonight. Sometimes she flew straight for the nearest star, but this night, she had gone in circles, never straying far from the village that was the only home she had ever known.

She looked down on the collection of huts that always looked so small from the skies. So foolish of the people living there to think they could hold off a winter storm or the fury of the mountains, and yet they had. There had been a village in this valley for as long as anyone could remember.

She dipped down again. Perhaps she should head in. Get some sleep on this midwinter's night. The healers would be called on in the morning, heads hurting from too much mead, and Gran's bones weren't as spry as they once were.

But as sensible as that sounded, Jae knew, somehow, that the stars didn't agree. They tugged at her feathers. Pushed the wind under her wings, chasing her higher on a draft that wasn't one she knew.

She frowned. She knew all the winds of these mountains, even the stormy, cantankerous ones.

A star, bright between two mountain peaks, caught her attention. It shone brighter and brighter until it was all she could look at.

And it spoke. *Your life here is done. Come.*

Jae could feel herself jerking. Flailing. Tangled in strange words in the sky that should not exist. Some part of her head, the part raised by Gran, knew this was foolishness. A figment or a demon, reaching for her through the winter storms.

But it didn't feel like a demon. It felt warm, like the star saw through to her very heart and did not find her strange.

Strange matters not. You are just as you are meant to be.

It took everything in Jae not to fly toward those words. To their warmth. To their impossible sense that Jae was somehow not other. "Gran waits for me." She spoke the words out loud, trying to fight the fearsome hold the bright star had on her heart.

The wind whipped away her words.

"I can't leave. I'm needed here." Even as she said the words and dipped once more toward the village, Jae knew she spoke lies. Mellie was at least as good a healer, and the villagers trusted her.

Brews worked better when the one who offered them was loved without reservation.

There is one waiting for you.

The words pierced her, claws to her chest. No one ever waited for her. Not like Mellie's man waited at the end of the day for his bride to come home. Not like the littles of the village waited for strong arms to pick them up and toss them into the sky and catch them again.

This wasn't right. Everyone knew only evil treachery made promises like this. Jae flapped her wings hard, fighting the gusts. She pointed straight to the village, resisting the call of the demon star.

You are needed.

Jae gasped. She couldn't leave. This was her home. And it was the middle of winter. She would never make it over the passes.

You will. I will lead you where you need to go.

Jae squeezed her eyes shut and aimed straight for the tree with her cloak and her bindings. The place where she could put her feet back on the ground and run away from whatever tried to pull her across the night sky.

The pull stopped.

Jae spun around, nearly stopping in midair. The star

still shone, and if she listened very carefully, she could still hear it calling.

But it wasn't making her go.

She felt her stomach trying to heave up her dinner. Demons didn't give choices.

Not a demon. Only a star.

Jae had no idea what to do. She was just a simple mountain healer.

The winds stopped, utterly silent—and a single thought whispered into the silence.

She is lonely too.

Jae's eyes squeezed closed, her mind listing off all the reasons why she couldn't go, starting with talking stars and ending with the practicalities of freezing to death before she got past the first mountain pass.

But it wasn't any of those thoughts that decided her. It was what she saw when the silence tugged her eyes back open.

A tiny figure on the ground, standing in the patch of snow behind her cozy hut, her cloak swirling in the night wind.

Gran.

Waving goodbye.

CHAPTER 2

She could hear the dragonets. Feel them. Queen bonds weren't supposed to happen until you were actually queen, but Fendellen had felt Lotus hatch, and she could feel these three working their way out of their shells too.

Which had worried her until Afran sent word. Elhen was fine.

Fendellen winged faster. The little ones called, and while there would be many to greet their arrival, the chance to watch three new dragons enter the world had kept her flying all the day and most of the night, too.

Irin would be cranky. Eggs somehow never managed to hatch on a bright summer afternoon. They picked midwinter nights and impending storms.

At least these three weren't up in the crook of some tree.

Three. It wasn't the number she'd been expecting.

They had three already chosen of the Dragon Star, and two more would have fulfilled the prophecy nicely. But apparently the sensibilities of mere queens-to-be were not the ones that mattered.

Fendellen snorted into the dark and bitter cold. On this night, even the Dragon Star ruled very little. Hatchlings took orders from no one.

She could feel it now, off in the distance. She couldn't yet spy the shape of the rocks and hills that marked the village for those who knew where to look—the snow swirled and obscured anything she might have seen, even if it weren't so blasted dark. But the village called her home all the same. Or perhaps a man and his dragon did.

Irin and Kis would be busy keeping the nursery rondo warm and ready for the three new arrivals and scorching anyone foolish enough to disturb the eggs, but they always managed to find a scratch under the chin and a bowl of milk curds when she arrived. Those were probably things a grown dragon and future queen shouldn't still covet, but she'd never been one to follow the rules overmuch.

She dropped her nose, flying under a particularly tangled swirl of air currents and snow. On this longest night, an arrow-straight line was definitely not the fastest path. The winds had been wreaking havoc with her wings for hours, and if truth must be known, she was tired.

She snorted, a mix of smoky happiness and relief, as the familiar rounded shape of one of the village's rondos emerged from the stormy dark. It wasn't the one she sought, but a quick turn, a dance of wings and snow, and she was on the ground right outside the nursery door. Not a landing normally permitted in the village, but on this night, there was no one outside to see her misbehavior.

Or so she thought until a well-wrapped figure dashed toward her in the snow. "Fendellen!" A mouth and two dark eyes emerged from the layers of wool. "Kis said you were nearly here. I've got meat pies inside for you. And milk curds."

Fendellen's chest squeezed. She offered up a wish, future queen to Dragon Star, that Kellan would get her heart's desire this night. There would be three hatchlings, and dragonets sometimes bonded as soon as they emerged. Not often, but if there was an elf who deserved the unusual, it was this one. "Thank you. No one makes better meat pies. I've been tasting them half the night."

Kellan giggled and pushed open the large door to the rondo, the one big enough to admit a somewhat bedraggled dragon and the snow she was bringing in with her.

Irin turned from the three eggs nestled in fresh straw right in front of Kis's nose. "Still tracking muddy footprints through my house, are you, missy?"

Fendellen knew most saw the weapons master and keeper of the nursery as abrasive and abrupt, but she'd learned to hear the caring under his words long ago. "There's not a speck of mud on me. Some snow, perhaps. Blame the new littles for that. It's not my fault they chose to hatch on such a miserable night."

His cheek twitched in that way it did when he was amused. "You've come to teach them to be good and proper hatchlings, have you?"

The rondo was crowded with villagers, most of them

seated respectfully, but several laughed at Irin's words. She snorted, careful to keep the smoke to a minimum. It was good to know her reputation in the village hadn't dimmed in her absence.

"It's good you're here," said a quiet voice at her side. "Kis has been sending to Elhen so that the rest of the dragons might see, but he tires."

Fendellen shot Karis a look. "These eggs would normally hatch in the forest where all could watch." A rondo couldn't begin to hold all the dragons who called the village home.

Karis nodded quietly. "Irin didn't want any babies lost in the forest."

More likely, he didn't want their old and proud queen standing in a winter storm for hours awaiting their arrival.

::You'll be clearing that thought from your mind before you speak with Elhen, missy.:: Kis sounded crankier than usual. Karis was right. He was tired. There was more than one dragon who shouldn't be out in the storms this night.

Fendellen dropped her nose, honoring the old dragon with heart and scales of gold. ::Let me send to the rest, old man. I could use the practice.::

He snorted, which caused one of the eggs to rock.

They all stared.

Fendellen let her gaze travel the room and reached for the connection with her queen that would let her send this waking vision to all.

::You're there. Good.:: Elhen sounded warm and comfortable.

Fendellen smelled a meat pie under her nose and swiped at it with her tongue, never taking her eyes off the eggs. She would never hear the end of it if the dragons in their caves on the cliffs missed the hatching because she was eating her dinner. She licked the hand under her tongue for good measure. Kellan, by taste and giggle.

Good. They awaited news of more than one kind this night, and a queen-to-be would do what she could to distract all of those who waited most impatiently. It wouldn't be long now. The egg that had rocked first had also set one of its neighbors into motion. Less wildly, but she could already see a crack making its way up that shell.

Some dragonets were all legs and motion. That one was smart.

::Indeed.:: Afran sounded as proud as if he was inside the shell offering directions to the tiny, wet dragon form struggling to find his or her way out.

Fendellen shook her head, amused, and kept her eyes on the third egg too. It hadn't so much as wiggled, but that didn't mean nothing was happening. She had emerged in a whirlwind of rocking and kicking and screeching cries, but lore had it that Afran had simply stuck his head out of a perfectly still shell.

::I believe it was his tail,:: Elhen said primly.

Fendellen tried hard not to laugh, but it had been a very long day and night, and her queen was making jokes.

The entire rondo shushed her—and then silence fell, pin-drop quiet, as one clawed foot thrust out into the light, dark purple and gleaming, claws scrabbling on air. A moment later, a great yellow head descended. Kis hovered, entirely still, as razor-sharp dragonet claws dug in and used the most sensitive skin of his nose as leverage. Fendellen could see the other powerful back leg now, pushing out beside the first.

One dragonet, coming out feet and tail first.

The second one wasn't, though. The entirely still egg had a nose poking up through the very top. Black, dark as Afran, and apparently just as wise. One claw delicately slid up beside the tiny, wet nose and expanded the opening. A second claw pushed through and a fine crack ran down the side of the egg, splitting and then splitting again like a stream running off the mountains.

Fendellen could feel the awe of the watching dragons. New life never got old, no matter how many times you bore witness.

::Indeed.:: Elhen's voice was hushed and a little wistful. ::You'll see these ones grow into fine young dragons.::

A shiver touched Fendellen's heart. ::I'll be off gallivanting. You're their queen.::

::For a while yet.:: A pause. ::Come talk to me in the next days. We will speak of your travels.::

That sounded vaguely ominous, but Fendellen couldn't concern herself with the words of queens. Not when the first egg had just exploded, sending shards of shell as far away as Irin's leather vest. The dark-purple dragonet worked her head out last, shaking the gooey snot that had kept her safe for months everywhere.

A tongue reached out to help with that, one nearly big enough to drown her head and that of the tiny black dragon as well. Kis, cleaning his new charges.

Fendellen kept her eyes on the last egg, the one in the middle that had done no more than rock gently. It tugged on her. It wasn't uncommon for one to take longer to hatch, but this one was somehow more than that.

::It is.:: Elhen's words were gentle. Almost reverent. ::Watch.::

As if they had heard their queen's voice, a purple head and a black one turned and faced the egg in between them. A black claw reached out and tapped, sending a fine crack racing through the intact egg. The tiny dark-purple hatchling leaned over to see, which only succeeded in knocking them both down.

The gathered crowd laughed softly at their antics, but Fendellen stayed quiet. They weren't playing. She could sense their purpose.

Two tiny, still-wet hatchlings got back onto their feet—and then, with teamwork much larger dragons could learn from, they attacked the egg. There was no other word for it. They worked fast and furiously, punching holes and tearing away shell.

::Is something wrong?:: Fendellen sent a very narrow message to Kis. He would know.

::No.:: The old dragon sounded like Elhen. Awed.

Moments later, the third dragonet's head was freed.

Fendellen felt her insides melt. The little one exactly matched the old dragon licking off her head. Scales of shiny gold.

The other two dragonets, minutes older and wiser, pulled off bits of shell and contributed slurping tongues to the job of cleaning off their younger nestling.

Which was when Fendellen finally saw. And understood.

The small golden baby had only stumps where her

front legs should have been, and eye crests so uneven, she almost looked squashed.

The villagers stirred, disturbed. Concerned.

Their murmurs barely registered. Fendellen felt the sweeping joy from the gathered dragons, inside and out, the awareness that they had been gifted this midwinter night with something far beyond a simple hatching.

::A special one.:: Elhen put words to what they could all feel and see.

Fendellen's heart swelled as two darker heads leaned in to the misshapen yellow one. ::And her guardians.::

::Yes. I had wondered.::

Three eggs. Now they knew why. The special ones came only rarely—and they never arrived alone.

Irin tilted his head as he sometimes did when he was listening to his dragon, and then he crouched down in front of the three. "Bonding to each other, are you? That's bound to be trouble."

The villagers relaxed. If the weapons master had no concerns, this was nothing to fear.

Fendellen was not worried. Special ones were revered by the dragons, and all in the village would learn soon enough how their scaled friends felt about the tiny yellow hatchling. She would live a good life, safe and honored and cherished, with two friends at her side.

Two bonded friends. Irin wasn't wrong about that. The three would be kin to each other. There would be no elves finding their dragons tonight. Fendellen turned her head, seeking one particular elf. She spied Kellan over on the side of the rondo, tucked out of the way of the villagers jostling for a better view. The small elf wore every emotion on her face. Joy. Commitment. Diligence. Yearning.

And sad understanding.

Surrounded by love and a deep part of it—and still apart.

Fendellen knew all too well how that felt.

CHAPTER 3

*J*ae slid along the long wall of the inn's main room, creeping a tiny bit closer to the fire. A few had noticed her in the shadows, but a young face wrapped in a worn blanket wasn't worthy of much notice.

She shivered. Even for one who rarely felt the cold, three nights of flying through midwinter storms and huddling in whatever shelter she could find during the day had left even the marrow of her bones frozen. The blanket, one she had found in the corner of an abandoned hut, did little to warm her, but it did cover her wings.

Leaving without at least her cloak and binding cloths had been foolishness beyond measure, but she had been caught up in promises whispered on the harsh winter wind.

The man with the gittern sitting on a stool by the fire sang of another just as foolish. An elf, leaving the warmth of home and clan to go find a fierce creature in the mountains. One with scales and wings and breath of fire, and big enough to block all the light of the sun from the world.

Jae let the pretty notes of the gittern wash over her and ease her homesickness a little. Gran told tales on the nights when winter had not yet begun to turn into spring, and Jae had always liked stories of the dragons, even if she had no scales or breath of fire.

"Cold, miss?" A voice at her shoulder startled her out of her listening. Another young woman like herself, with wild curls escaping her tidy bun and a calm, easy voice. "Ma said to bring you a cup of tea."

Jae winced. She shouldn't have come in, but she'd heard the music as she flew over the tiny inn, and even the call of the star hadn't been able to keep her in the sky. "I'm sorry. I have no money to pay. I'll go now."

"Ach." The young woman shrugged and gave a friendly grin. "Half of what's in here has no money, and the tea's mostly hot water anyhow. Minstrel's more likely to come back if we fill the room, so you might as well stay."

There was kindness in the words, more than Jae had heard in three days. She reached for the chipped and well-used mug, keeping her wings carefully tucked behind her. "Thank you." She wanted, very much, to see if an offer to sweep or bake bread in the morning might earn her a place to sleep by the fire, but even a blanket wouldn't hide her wings in the light of day. Instead, she turned away from curious, friendly eyes. Questions would only lead to danger, and she'd already risked enough of that leaving the safety of the skies.

The young woman walked off, her attention already

shifting to a noisy group in the corner waving their cups in the air. Ones with money, perhaps—or familiarity.

Jae's heart squeezed again. She'd never gone three days without a familiar face. The very few people she'd seen on this precipitous, ill-planned trip had regarded her with grave suspicion, although that was perhaps not a surprise. Very few traveled in mid-winter, and even fewer did so alone with little more than a wool blanket to call their own.

Her stomach grumbled, and she took a sip of the tea. It was mostly water, as promised, but there were hints of a few herbs. The warmth soothed her belly, although it wouldn't fool it for very long. She'd foraged some, but the abandoned kitchen garden of two days back was a distant memory, and even a healer used to finding edibles in the wild found slim pickings in snow up to her knees. In the mountains, there were small streams, banks steep enough not to freeze, that would feed a hungry belly even in winter, but the lands she flew over were flatter now, and she knew far less about how to feed herself.

She wrapped a hand around her stomach as it grumbled more loudly. She didn't want attention. She only wanted to listen to the music for another song or two and then she'd make her way back to the door and the cold, crisp night sky. The storm had finally blown over, and it would be clear flying tonight.

Straight toward a star.

She felt the tears gathering in her eyes, but she blinked them away fiercely. She was on a fool's errand, but she could still feel the pull inside her ribs. The one that said she must do this crazy thing even if it led it straight into death, and not the kind that minstrels would sit by the fire and sing about one day.

She would simply be another body found in the spring melts. If she was fortunate, someone would cover her with rocks to mark her passing. She helped make such cairns after every winter. The high mountains were not kind to the puny humans who walked their craggy passes and fished in their streams and built huts and birthed babies in their shadows.

The minstrel finished his song and reached for the mug of ale set on a nearby stool. The chatter in the room swelled, filling the space his music had once claimed. Jae shrank deeper into the walls. Eyes not turned to the fire were more likely to see her in the shadows.

"Hungry?" The voice was male this time. A man, seated, with the permanently sun-stained skin and deep wrinkles of the high mountains. He held up a bowl with a half-chunk of bread and some stew soppings still in the bottom. "All y'orn if you clear the bowl after."

She would have to step out of the shadows to take it— and there were other hungry eyes that had turned toward his offer. She shook her head and shrank back. "No, thank you." She held up her mug, hoping he would think it contained rich broth or thick tea. Something that justified turning down the first warm food she'd laid eyes on in days.

He eyed her a moment longer and then swiped the bread around the bowl himself.

She turned toward the minstrel, sending a silent, fervent wish that he might start playing again. He didn't seem so inclined—he laughed with those sitting close to the fire, tipping back his ale to drink deeply.

She wrapped the blanket tighter around herself and eased a step backward toward the door. She'd overstayed her welcome, and now that the music was gone, its pull on her had vanished too. She could feel the star tugging on her. Calling her out into the night with nothing more than a musty blanket around her shoulders.

When the songs and tales spoke of trials, they never mentioned smelling bad. Or how weak her wings felt after three days of not enough to eat. She eased another step backward. The mountain man's eyes raked over her again, but he seemed to be the only one looking. She let the cuffs of her dress slip out of the blanket. She didn't look like a lass who had grown up on the high slopes, but the embroidery on her cuffs would tell the story of her village to one who knew how to read the simple, colorful stitches.

Put there in case her body was one of the ones found in the spring.

Not this far from home, though. No one else in the room had such stitching on their cuffs and collars. If she died in these parts, she would be wearing a message no one knew how to read. She flinched and took another step back. Her eyes strayed to the mountain man one last time. He was a stranger, but he had the look of home. Perhaps the last one she would ever see.

She blinked back tears. She wanted to go home. Had tried, more times than she knew how to count. But always, when she did, the feeling in her chest stretched taut, like the only way to go back to her village was to leave her heart beating in the sky behind her.

A hiss.

Jae spun toward the sound, and this face was neither familiar nor friendly. A woman, large as any man, seated on a stool and staring at the floor.

Jae looked down and froze in horror. The edge of her wing trailed through the dirt and grime. Feathers she hadn't bound because she was too weary to find a cloth that might do the job.

She tried to think. Predators in the forest smelled fear, and so did ones in villages. It was best to act like you were meant to be just as you were. "It's no creature, miss. Have no fear. Where I'm from, we use the feathers of birds to line our skirts."

Skeptical blue eyes lifted to hers. "I'm no miss, and whoever you are, you're a long way from home."

Jae wanted nothing more than to pull the blanket tighter around her shoulders, but she resisted. Loose like it was, perhaps the woman wouldn't notice the humps on her back. Or perhaps, in the dark, she would think them a cloak. "I am. And leaving just now."

The doubt in the blue eyes deepened. "It's the dead of night. No one's leaving now unless they've thieved something."

Jae had no earthly idea what she might have stolen that came with feathers and lumps, but it didn't matter. Thieves never met good ends. "I don't steal."

"Then you have some explaining to do." The large woman reached for the knife at her side.

Jae had seen that look before, from the occasional traveler to her village. A few might offer her an initial kindness, but as soon as they saw what she was, fear landed.

Danger. The village had known her as a babe. No one meeting her fully grown ever saw her as anything other than dangerous.

And dangerous things met knives all too often.

Jae backed up faster, keeping her wings to the shadows as best as she could.

She heaved a teary sigh of relief when the sounds of the gittern rang through the room. The woman shot her one last dirty look and turned to face the fire, clearly deciding she had better things to do than chase a petty thief on a cold winter's night.

Something she might easily change her mind about if she knew what those dirty feathers were really attached to.

Jae swallowed. No matter how lonely she had felt in her small village, it was far worse here, in a room full of people who could turn in an instant. To belong only because she was Gran's was bad enough. Out here in the wider world, she could never belong at all.

Jae set her mug down gently on the corner of a table. It hurt to leave the still-warm tea, and the song the minstrel had just started was one of her favorites. But whatever demon had possessed her clearly didn't care.

It wanted her to die of cold instead of loneliness.

She slipped out the door into the dark night and swallowed back her tears. Out here, they would only freeze to her face.

CHAPTER 4

Fendellen settled onto the visitor cushions in the dim-dark cave and tried not to squirm. Morning had come, with new-fallen snow to her knees, three sleeping hatchlings and a very sleepy village, and a summons.

"Relax and finish your stew. I promised young Kellan you would eat."

Queens rarely made simple promises. However, the stew smelled delightful, and if Kellan chose to tend to her own heart by taking care of others, that was something a dragon who would one day be queen would honor as well as she could. Fendellen dipped her tongue into the sauce of the stew, appreciating the flavors. Elhen had a fondness for exotic tastes, and dragons returning from their travels often brought back spices to please their queen.

Ones who had a little warning they were returning, anyhow.

Fendellen kept quiet and made quick work of her stew.

Elhen's patience had increased in her later years, but that didn't mean it was endless, particularly where her successor was concerned. And while this might not have the trappings of a formal visit, she doubted it was one meant merely for stew and idle conversation either.

The queen waited until she was licking the very last of the fragrant meal from the bottom of the bowl. "It is time for your questing to end."

Fendellen hid a sigh. She had heard such pronouncements before, and not everyone used such kind words to describe her traveling hijinks. "My queen is still hale and hearty, and I still need to grow in wisdom."

That earned her a snort. "The latter half, I will grant you. The state of your queen's health is perhaps less certain. I am nearly old enough to see through."

Worried blue eyes looked up to find the deep green ones that were all that still held color on the old queen's body.

Elhen shook her head. "I know of no troubles that seek me other than old age. Fret not. I am not yet ready to go, although the star doesn't always wait for us to be ready."

Fendellen was quite sure that last pronouncement was intended to do double duty, but it wasn't her own readiness to be queen she doubted. It was something simpler than that, and always had been. "It's not time." She knew that as surely as she knew her own name.

"So you have always said, youngling." Green eyes gentled. "You have a deeper connection to the star than most. But I do not speak of the day you become queen. You must stay and give the dragons more time to know you. There are some who have heard only stories of the ice-blue dragon and her travels, and you cannot be the queen of dragonkind based only on stories."

It wasn't quite that dire—and more than one queen had started her reign with little more than that. But Elhen's message was more serious. "You think I shirk my duties."

"I think you entirely redefine them." The queen's voice was dry.

Fendellen tried, once again, not to squirm. It was hard to hide when the dragon she faced had watched her hatch.

"There is change coming. The prophecy, and perhaps more. I do what I feel is necessary. What the star requires of me."

A long pause. "Do you?"

This time, there was no hiding her unease. "I try."

A long, smoky sigh. "Talk to me, youngling. There is no one else who would understand, but while I may seem older than the hills, I remember being a brash young dragon once."

Fendellen shaped a sharp memory of a certain translucent tail, splashing into the waters of midsummer and soaking a large yellow dragon, and sent it to her queen.

Elhen's rumbled laughter filled the cave. "Perhaps a taste of that brashness still remains."

Hopefully for a long time to come. "I will be ready when I need to be." Brave words. Some days, she even believed them, although this one, even filled with sleepy celebration and very good stew, didn't feel like one of them.

Another long pause, and the steady gaze of eyes that had seen everything for a very long time. "Tell me what you wait for."

Fendellen closed her eyes. Her queen had spoken, and she would look at that place deep inside herself that had always known, but did not always have words. ::There is a part of me that is empty. That waits. I do not believe I can be queen until it is filled.::

::Fear speaks thusly.::

The words were gentle—and piercing. But it wasn't fear that lived deep in Fendellen, or not only that. It was truth. To be queen was to be entirely alone. Even Kis treated Elhen with a respect, a distance. She wasn't ready to take that last step into loneliness. Not until she had filled her empty places. ::I travel to find what fills me.::

Elhen sounded amused. ::Spices from far-flung lands are wondrous, but they are not the answer to all things.::

Fendellen snorted. The queen had a wry humor to go along with her volatile temper and haughty ways. "It's more than my belly that sits empty."

A white head finally nodded in the dim. "You are a different dragon than I was at your age. I was much like young Alonia and Trift. It was responsibility I feared."

Those two knew how to have more fun in an hour in the forest than most knew how to have in a lifetime, and Fendellen loved them dearly for it. But it wasn't responsibility she feared. It was the great, gaping chasm between the queen and everyone else. "The star chose them, as it chooses us." A rebuke, as carefully put as she could make it.

Elhen's eyes glittered diamond hard, and then with a humor few ever saw. "I am not fond of trusting the destiny of dragonkind to the stars, youngling. You would do well to cultivate your own wisdom in that regard."

That was hard to do when you were going to be queen in an era of prophecies fulfilled. "Three have been chosen. We await two more."

A thoughtful look. "You have the bonds of a queen with those three already."

Fendellen was beyond tired of needing to squirm, but that fact hadn't escaped her notice either. "I feel them deeply, but I am not yet their queen. They know it, as do I."

Elhen snorted. "I don't accuse you of usurping my authority. I wonder if perhaps the missing two are the source of your emptiness, and the blood of the queens inside you simply lacks the words and the understanding to know that as the cause."

Fendellen blinked. It was an interesting thought. Despite her sharp fear of loneliness, she had never actually lacked for dragon companionship. An old yellow dragon who treated her like a hatchling had always ensured that. No queens-to-be were treated with reverence or distance on his watch. It was an odd thought that the emptiness inside her might be bonds that did not yet exist, rather than experiences.

An interesting thought, and one she refused to think about any longer. She was a dragon of action, not one who grew wisdom slowly in the forest like a mushroom. And while Elhen had not yet issued an order, it was quite clear there was one forthcoming. "I will stay for a while. The remainder of the winter, perhaps."

Amusement glinted in green eyes. "There are three hatchlings who would do well to know their future queen."

Fendellen let her own amusement glint back. "Kis might not want my influence on his charges."

"That old warrior has dealt with far tougher than you." Elhen paused. "And it would do well for the villagers to see your reverence."

They no longer talked about the travel plans of ice-blue dragons. "The special one."

"Yes. Elf clans do better than human villages, but both would see such a one as a burden, a mouth demanding more food and more care and giving little in return."

Dragons did no such accounting. "She honors us with her presence."

"I know that, and any elf or human kin to a dragon knows it by now as well." Elhen raised her head, a regal queen on full display. "It is well that the others have a good example to follow."

There were few things Fendellen liked less than being an example, but for that squished yellow head, she would do anything that was necessary. "Do you truly think it a concern?"

The barest of head shakes. "I do not know. They accept a dragon who swims, but there is distance still."

Distance that was as much Oceana's fault as anyone else's. "Kis is well loved."

"Kis is a hero." Four words spoken directly from the banked fire of a queen.

Fendellen bowed her head. Messages received.

All of them.

CHAPTER 5

*J*ae glared up at the night sky. Her feet were frozen solid, her cheeks flayed by wind until she couldn't feel them anymore. "I will not. I'm done. I'm going home."

The tug of the star pulsed in her ribs.

She didn't care. Five days and five nights, and even her ribs had turned to ice. She was so far beyond hungry, she could no longer remember food, and she'd been chased off twice in two days by people hurling stones and nocking arrows as they screamed words she didn't understand.

She is close.

Jae wrapped her wings around her body and wished she had the power to yank the star out of the sky, tie it off to the biggest rock she could find, and hurl it down some crevice with no bottom. Which might be hard to find in these flat lands, but she would do it as her last living act if it would only bring her some peace.

Your life will not be peaceful. But it will soon be warm.

Jae used words Gran would have gaped at. She moved the icy blocks that used to be her feet, turning around on the hard-packed snow, painfully slow.

Facing home.

She would take to the sky one more time. Perhaps, if she was very lucky, she would fall out of the sky close enough to the mountains that in spring, someone would recognize the stitching on her cuffs and send word back to Gran.

Assuming Gran was still alive. The shadow waving from outside the hut must have been the work of demons too. Jae felt the tears she could no longer stop spill over her cheeks. They rolled, cold and stinging, and turned to ice, yet more evidence of just how little warmth was left in her body.

She had made such a terrible mistake. She was not understood in her village—but she was not hated either. Even if death didn't stalk her, in these lands, her heart would be forever as cold as her feet. Ignored at best, chased and arrow-shot at worst.

There will be no arrows this night. Fly.

No one was dumb enough to waste precious arrows shooting at sky shadows in the dark. Jae spread her wings, feeling the numbness creeping even under her feathers.

She would fly—but she would go home.

~

*R*estless. So very, ridiculously restless. Fendellen winged up into the night sky, glaring at the star that had pulled her away from sleep. ::I know these long nights must be boring for you with so little to watch, but I was up all day with a small purple dragonet who hatched without knowing what sleep is, so I was really looking forward to a nap.::

She caught a crisp updraft and snorted into the stiff wind. Talking to a star was a sure sign she'd been awake far too long. Especially when it sounded very much like the star was laughing. Fendellen flapped hard, climbing at a pitch that would have challenged all but a few. It wasn't any warmer up high, but the view was better. It was fun to pretend to be one of the stars rather than part of the landscape they hung over and occasionally mocked.

She surveyed the dark, feeling out the air currents with her wings. On a night this cold, it was always tempting to head toward the sea and its warm updrafts, but something niggled, tugging her a different direction.

She executed a barrel roll that would have done Lotus proud and pointed her nose toward the niggling. The lands below weren't ones dragons generally flew over. Too many fields, and the humans who tended them might not take kindly to a flyover by a large winged creature. However, there would be no field tending this night. The fields hid under blankets of deep snow, and humans didn't have scales and bellies full of fire to keep them warm.

She studied the horizon ahead. There were mountains this way, more distant than her eyes could see, but she had flown in their direction more than once. They were beautiful in the summer, full of brave flowers that bloomed only briefly and were somehow more dazzling because of it. But even in summer, those mountains gave birth to fierce storms, and in winter, even restless dragon queens would do well to stay far away.

Fendellen stretched her wing tips, arcing in a wide circle. She huffed an amused puff as a dragon-shaped shadow caught the light of the moon and reflected on the snow below. It was a pretty shadow. She flapped her wings, not because it was necessary, but because it was fun to watch the shadow dragon flap too.

~

*J*ae blinked her eyes as the impossible flying creature dipped her wings again, dancing with the shadow on the snow. The old ones had spoken of such things—the torments of the mind that came just before death. Somehow, she had expected them to be less playful.

Somewhere, deep in the cold inside her, she felt a struggling heat, something that might have finished as a smile on a night when she wasn't encased in ice. One of her wings twitched, wanting to join the dance in the sky.

Jae didn't move. If she did, surely the illusion would vanish, and at least this way, she could die watching something so beautiful it nearly made her cold heart stop.

Moonlight shone off the dragon's scales. They weren't quite white. A touch of blue, like the most beautiful ice on the lakes in the high mountains, the ones born from rocks and ice.

Starlight with wings.

Jae's breath huffed out into the night, and with it, the

faintest of sounds. A whimper, dying as fast as it was born. A wish that lacked enough flame to find its voice.

The dragon's wings froze.

Somehow, the beautiful demon had heard her.

Jae knew she should run. Pray. Hide. Something. Anything other than standing there, staring at the sky as deep blue eyes searched the shadows and star-bright wings flapped straight at where she stood.

But it would make no difference. There was no escaping the cliffs of snow that sometimes broke off a mountain and raced down, killing everything they touched, and there was no escaping this.

Jae felt her knees shaking, trying to falter, but they were too cold to bend and let her fall to the snow. So she stood, a frozen stick, as wings blasted air past her ears and landed a dragon right in front of her face.

The very last thing she remembered were starlight eyes.

~

The girl was cold. So very, terrifyingly cold.

Fendellen swept her up in claws and forelegs, not at all certain why there were so many lumps under the worn blanket and not caring. She had seen humans close to death, but she had never seen one this close who was still standing. She tucked the waif, mostly skin and bones and not much bigger than Kellan, against her chest scales and lifted into the sky. There were ways to warm a body, but none of them worked in the dead of night in a field of snow and shadows.

She needed a cave.

The village was too far away, and it wasn't the right answer anyhow. The girl was hers to protect, a bone-deep knowledge Fendellen didn't question. She accepted. There was no other choice. What she had seen in those green-gray eyes before they had fluttered shut in an ice-white face had been impossible—and entirely certain.

The frail, frozen stick of a human she carried was her kin.

She pointed straight for the star that had somehow known she was needed this night. There were rocky hills close by, if she could find them in the snow.

The sky murmured. A little this way. A little more that.

Fendellen followed, letting the message in the stars speak to the part of her that would one day be queen. The rest of her tried to curl around the cold body she carried, willing her fire into a belly that didn't know how to hold heat in this cold.

The wind yanked away the blanket, and every thought in Fendellen's head shattered and cracked on the snow below. Not human. The being she carried had wings. White, feathered ones that wrapped around her, even now, struggling to reshape themselves against the wind.

A whimper broke through her shock.

::Hold on. I'm taking you somewhere I can make nice and warm.:: Fendellen somehow formed the words despite the sense that she had somehow fallen into a dream and couldn't find her way out. Humans didn't fly. Then again, they didn't generally turn to ice under starry skies, either. She glared up at the Dragon Star. ::You might have taken better care of her. Humans are more fragile than dragons.::

Sadness. Worry.

Fendellen blinked. Stars did not regret.

Another whimper. ::C-c-cold.::

How a mind so frozen could form any words at all was a mystery. One they could solve later. Fendellen spied a misshapen tree that marked the edge of the rocky hills. There were caves there. One she remembered in particular with a small spring inside.

She put more will into her wings. Elves liked the hot waters of Oceana's pool. Perhaps a human girl would too. ::You will be warm soon. It is not much farther.::

::Nice demon.::

Fendellen's heart lurched. The very ill sometimes had waking dreams where they saw things that weren't real. Things of nightmare. ::No demons come for you. Not while I watch. I will keep you safe.::

It felt like the most important promise of her life.

CHAPTER 6

*I*t was warm.

She must be dead.

Jae struggled to open her eyes. They felt as heavy as midwinter snowpack, like opening them might require an entire village with ropes and shovels and strong backs.

::Be easy. You shiver yet.::

The snowpack blasted away as her eyes yanked themselves open. She stared at the head she could barely see in the shadows, and her very strange dream came flooding back. The one where a dragon demon had landed from the sky.

::I am no demon. Just a dragon.::

The head came a little closer, and Jae could see moonlight glistening off scales the color of high-mountain lake ice. She pushed up onto her arms, which felt like the gangly legs of newborn goats.

A warm nose nudged her up to sitting.

Jae shook her addled head. Demons were never kind in

the stories Gran told. Dragons mostly weren't either. And none of them ever kidnapped half-dead mountain girls and took them to caves for any good reason. She looked around. It was definitely a cave. Small and filled with moonlight and somehow still warm. Even if she could figure out how to get her legs working well enough to escape, leaving the warmth that she could feel seeping into her frozen bones didn't seem like a good idea at all. She could feel the colder air toward the mouth of the cave.

Wherever the dragon had brought her, it was still winter.

::If you sit against my side under my wing, I can keep you warmer.::

Jae shook, and not only from the cold. Hearing voices inside her head was eerie. First a star, and now a dragon. Perhaps she was dead after all.

::It is quite normal for dragons to talk to their kin this way.:: A long pause. ::I did not know the star had talked to you.::

Some of the fog left Jae's head. She stared at the eyes that were the brightest thing in the cave. "The star talks to you, too?"

A long blink. ::On occasion. But I have never heard of it talking to humans before.::

Five days of pure misery rose up in Jae's throat. "It told me to leave home and fly through the dark and it kept insisting, even when I wanted to turn around and go back, or just lie down and die where they would understand the stitching on my cuffs and tell Gran when the spring melts came."

A low rumble filled the cave.

Jae scurried back against the cave wall.

The rumble abruptly ceased. ::I'm sorry. I would never do you harm. But I am angry at the star. It was not necessary to drag you away like this. I would have come to find you.::

Jae stared. "Why?"

The nose edged gingerly closer, like Jae sometimes did when she wanted to offer a berry to a wild creature. ::We are kin. We are meant for each other. It's a bond as powerful as mother to child or husband to wife.::

Jae's throat tightened. "My mother left me on the side of a mountain to die."

Her head filled with aching, wordless sorrow—and then with something far different. The same gentle sweetness she associated only with Gran. ::Ah. Perhaps I should have said grandmother to granddaughter, then. I am glad you have one who loves you.::

The waving figure in the snow pierced Jae's heart. "I left. She doesn't know why."

::We will send word. Does she know of dragons?::

Jae smiled. "Yes."

::Good. Then she will be proud you are kin to one.::

Jae gulped. None of this felt real, including the warmth. She shivered as a draft blew in the mouth of the cave.

The feelings in her head changed to something more practical. ::We need to get you warm, youngling. I'm afraid I can't do much to feed you until morning, but either come under my wing, or if you like, the water is warm. Some of the other dragon kin enjoy such things.::

Jae followed the direction of the demon-dragon's gaze

to a small pool of water in the back of the cave. A single stray wisp of moonlight shimmered on its surface.

A spring.

A *steaming* spring.

She gaped. There was one such in a small valley a fortnight's journey away from the village. Gran had taken her there in search of rare plants for healing, and to touch the sacred waters. That one was a tiny pool barely big enough for her hands. This one was larger than the trough they bathed in.

::That is what the others do. They put all of themselves in the water.::

Such a wonder could only be the offer of a demon, but Jae didn't care. The few baths she took were never anything more than lukewarm, wood to heat the water being in short supply in the high mountains. And her bones were so very cold. She looked down at her heavy woolen dress. It would not do to get it wet—it took forever and three more days to dry—but she had underthings she could bathe in.

She reached up to untie the part of her dress that looped around her wings—and froze. Her wings. She wore neither blanket nor cloak, nothing to keep her feathers hidden from the demon-dragon's eyes.

A grumble. ::You need to stop calling me a demon.::

Jae swallowed. It wouldn't do to make a demon mad, especially one that could hear her thoughts. ::What should I call you?::

A snort that sounded almost like laughter. ::I'm so sorry, youngling. My manners are terrible. I am Fendellen.:: A pause, and a stern feeling in her head, which she was beginning to understand came from the dragon.

::Your wings are beautiful. I'm sorry you've had to hide them.::

Jae stared.

::I have wings too. You might have noticed.::

Dragons were supposed to have wings. Humans weren't.

A nose nudged her toward the steaming pool. ::We can talk about that when your teeth have stopped chattering. Into the water with you.:: The nose stopped pushing on her. ::Will the water harm your feathers?::

Jae laughed. This was a strange and wondrous dream. ::No. They shed water just like a duck. They're really dirty, though.:: Somehow, that shamed her in a way that cold bones and a hungry belly had not.

::Of course they are.:: The nose nudged her again, and Jae reached up for the ties of her dress. ::You've been traveling, and we all look bedraggled when we've been on a journey.::

Such crisp kindness. Jae ducked her head, hoping the dream lasted long enough for Gran to meet her dragon. She had the feeling they would like each other.

~

*A*kin who thought she was both demon and dream fragment. Fendellen kept her snorts to herself. That would likely scare the poor girl, and she was swaying on her feet as it was. Instead, she borrowed from Irin's arsenal and stuck to the simple, pragmatic instructions Jae seemed to respond well to. They fit with the brisk, practical face in her kin's mind. The only source of uncomplicated love she had ever had in her life.

Fendellen frowned as the girl peeled off the last of her woolen layers and stood shivering in a linen shift, wrapping her dirty feathers around herself for warmth. Many arrived in the dragon kin village because their homes no longer wanted them, and Jae's story was better than many, but it pierced more deeply. This was her kin, and that she had grown up in fear and shadow, hiding so much of who she was, banged on Fendellen's ribs far harder than any sword. She nudged Jae toward the water. ::Test with your toe first, youngling. I may have made it overwarm.::

The girl dipped in a very tentative toe and then sighed, a long exhale of utter bliss. "It's perfect. Thank you." Very gingerly, she sat down on the edge of the pool and let her legs slide in.

Fendellen watched carefully. Sometimes human skin turned to frost, and then she would need to get Jae to a healer before morning, before anything could turn black and fall off. ::Does your skin tingle?::

Jae turned her head, eyes full of puzzlement—and curiosity. "Are you a healer, Fendellen?"

She said the last word like she was tasting a new food, but it was a different word that caught her dragon's attention. Suddenly some of the memories she had picked up from her kin's mind made more sense. "I'm not, but you are."

Jae shrugged, hugging her wings around her. "Gran's a healer. I'm one of her apprentices."

There was no healer in the village, but Irin and Karis knew enough to judge Jae's skill. For now, all Fendellen

54

wanted was to keep her safe. "You live in the high moun-tains. Can you tell if your skin needs special healing, or just warmth?"

Jae smiled a little. "I don't get frostbite. Usually I can fly on the coldest nights and be fine."

That was a relief—and a mystery. Jae was clearly more than a simple, ordinary human. One who didn't yet know that she was kin to more than a simple, ordinary dragon, but that wasn't something Fendellen intended to say this night. She'd be far too likely to end up a demon queen with a kin dead of terror. ::In the water, missy. All of you. Wings too.::

Jae slid in slowly, her toes tentatively reaching for the bottom. She gasped when she made it in all the way up to her chin, and then exhaled a sigh of utter bliss.

Fendellen felt the resonance of that down the kin bond and let go some of her own worry. They were away from the sharp edges of danger now. Everything else could be dealt with one step at a time.

Beginning with a soak in the pool.

Fendellen had never had a bath, but she had seen them. With a particularly dirty human or elf, there was normally a rinse before a proper bath, but there were no buckets around, and anyway, pouring water over her kin would be an act of torture, not one of friendship. She settled in by the pool. It didn't matter if her kin got clean. It mattered only that she was warm and happy.

The sun would rise in a few hours, and then they could make their way home.

Her chin got halfway to resting on her tail before the import of those words sank in. She had a kin who thought she was a demon. One who had grown up in a tiny village in the high mountains. She might never have met an elf before, never mind a dragon. Or seen a village of decent size, for that matter.

She glared out the mouth of the cave at the Dragon Star. ::Really? This is the kin you picked for one who will be queen?::

The star didn't answer, but Fendellen felt better for speaking anyhow. It wasn't for herself that she spoke, but for her kin. Jae needed love and time, not the hard walk that lay ahead.

Fendellen laid her chin down on her tail and pondered. Jae needed protection. Shielding. Perhaps in time, she would grow into the destiny the star had blithely assigned her, but if it landed too soon, it would freeze her to death or pluck all the feathers from her wings.

Something an ice-blue dragon refused to let happen.

She reached deep inside herself to the place where the power of all queens lived. It should still be dormant, awaiting Elhen's death, but it wasn't, and tonight was a very good time to test the full power of her reach. She considered a moment and then sent. ::Afran?:: Kis might be better, but he had three young charges, and she knew better than to disrupt the nursery at such a time.

A moment later, a touch answered in her mind, one tossing off the vestiges of sleep. ::Fendellen. Are the hatch-lings in danger?::

That would be the most obvious reason to rouse him in the night. ::No. I am in a cave two hours' flight from the village. With my kin.::

Silence—and then quiet, sincere delight. ::You are bonded.::

She was. And while there were some complications, she let herself bask in that delight. ::Yes. I found her half-frozen in the snow. I've brought her to a cave with a small pool and heated the water. She is recovering well from the cold.:: And half asleep, which Fendellen intended to watch carefully. She did not desire a dip in the pool herself, and she had already rescued her kin from the clutches of danger once this night.

::Two hours is not far. Do you need food or blankets?::

Fendellen studied the sky. The dawn was hours away yet, but Jae needed time yet before they left the cave. Time to warm a little more, and then to sleep. There was no need to pull others from their warm beds on such an icy night. ::No. I will bring her in the morning. Perhaps Inga could have a thick soup ready.:: Bellies that had not eaten for days did not do well with chunky stews.

::It will be done.:: Afran's voice was as calm as it ever was, but there was a hint of curiosity. Of waiting.

She knew the cause. He was feeling the unease of the one who would someday be his queen. ::I need you to tell the others. She is very new to the idea of dragons and kin. For now, I want to be treated as an ordinary dragon of the village. For us to be treated as an ordinary bonded pair.::

Blinking surprise. ::You don't wish for her to know you will be queen?::

Dragons didn't lie—that was a trait of elves and humans. But a future queen learned from everyone and used what she must. ::She believes me a demon, Afran. Let me tell her gently. As she is ready.::

Empathy. And firmness. ::None are ever ready.::

Perhaps not—but the future that awaited her kin was heavier than most. Fendellen stared at Jae's forehead and the mark that shone there. ::I would have her know joy before she knows of this.::

Chagrin. Quiet judgment.

Afran wasn't the most flexible of dragons. ::It is my choice to make, and I have made it.:: Jae needed to be free before she learned of the grave responsibilities that were now hers to carry.

A long silence. Acceptance. ::I will tell the others. Bring her in the morning. We will be ready.::

CHAPTER 7

*J*ae stood on the edge of the sheer cliff outside the mouth of the cave, staring at the new day. It wasn't early morning anymore. She had slept through that, an act which Gran never would have allowed. Only the sick and very elderly escaped morning chores.

Although she might have qualified as sick last night.

She looked over at the ice-blue dragon standing calmly on the cliffs beside her. Now that it was light and her teeth were no longer chattering, she could think more calmly. Demons didn't keep you warm at night and then wake you up and push you into another warm, steamy bath, this one far cleaner than the night before. Her wings fairly gleamed in the sunlight, and it was all Jae could do not to stretch them out and take to the skies.

An amused rumble beside her. ::We can fly, youngling. As soon as you're ready.::

Jae gulped. She hadn't flown in daylight since she was tiny. It caused too much fear.

::We will fly a route where no one is likely to see us from the ground.:: Fendellen, strong and sure. ::Dragons also stay out of sight when we must, but we do not shirk the sun. And the inhabitants of these lands close to our village are used to spotting a dragon or two.::

A dragon, perhaps. Not a human with wings. Nerves jangled in Jae's belly.

A warm nose touched her cheek. ::Trust, sweet one. These are my lands. I would not fly you into danger.::

That settled something deeper than Jae's belly. She reached up a hesitant hand, afraid to touch and needing to. Dragon scales were so beautiful in the light.

Fendellen arched her neck. ::All dragons like to be told we're pretty. And there is a place just above my eye crests that is always itchy.::

Jae jumped as a head nuzzled her, much like the goats did when they wanted to be petted. Very slowly, she let her fingers touch the skin over the eye ridge. It had no scales, just a leathery toughness.

It twitched under her fingers, and she jumped again.

::Touch like you mean it, youngling.:: Fendellen sounded greatly amused. ::Otherwise, it tickles.::

Dragons were ticklish? Jae's laughter squirted out into the noonday sun.

Fendellen gave her a glare that didn't look scary at all. ::You're going to be a troublesome kin, are you?::

Kin. Jae had no idea what to make of such an idea. Bonded to a dragon. It seemed like the stuff of dreams, but she could feel the truth of it inside her. Perhaps dragons needed servants, like the fancy ladies in far-off lands.

::Never.:: Fendellen sounded almost grim. ::A kin bond is a pairing of equals. You are not less.::

Jae shook her head, but she had no words. So she did as Gran always said to do when there were too many plants in the forest. Pick one at a time. She looked out over the vast expanse of snow beneath them. They would fly together, and then she would deal with whatever came after. She unfurled her feathers and shivered as the cold touched her skin.

::We can wait.:: Fendellen sounded worried, maybe even a little panicked. ::We can fly when it is warmer.::

Jae felt laughter bubbling up in her throat again. ::Then we will be stuck in that cave until spring and you will die of hunger. I heard your belly rumbling earlier.::

Fendellen looked chagrined. ::Others would bring us food.::

That was only for the elderly or very sick. ::My skin sometimes shivers in the wind, but I will tell you if I'm truly cold. Today I'm just very awake and excited.:: And nervous and stunned, but she was not a mouse. Whatever this was, she would meet it with her head high and make Gran proud.

A long silence. She could feel her dragon's eyes watching her. Then long, ice-blue wings unfurled, and a warm nose nudged her shoulders. ::To the skies, sweet one.::

Jae felt the bond between them tugging, almost a physical thing. ::You will come?::

::I will be right beside you.::

She felt the tears trying to brim over again and blinked them back. It would not do to freeze her cheeks. Even if this was only a very long and strange dream, to fly with another was a thought that made her shake with happiness.

The skies had always been her freedom—and the loneliest place on earth.

She tipped forward, her wings catching the updraft running up the cliff, letting it toss her into the sky.

She felt the surprise behind her, and the glee. A breath later, winds buffeted her as ice-blue dragon wings flapped just off the tip of her own feathered ones. ::That was a beautiful takeoff, youngling. Just like the eagles. I did not know such a thing was possible for a larger flier.::

Jae caught a new updraft, letting the sky carry her up on a current of pure, hot joy. ::I watch the mountain birds. It's how I learned.::

::Ah.:: Amusement again—and pride. ::The other dragons will spend much time trying to copy your smoothness.::

Jae stuttered and nearly fell out of the sky. ::Other dragons?::

::We go to the village,:: Fendellen said softly. ::Of dragons and their kin.::

She swallowed hard, not sure what was more frightening. ::Human kin?::

::A few. Mostly elves.:: A sharp prickle, like a porcupine had just sat down inside Jae's head. ::You will not fear them.::

She was far more worried they would fear her.

::We would never fear one who can fly so beautifully.::

Jae's wings stuttered again.

Off in the distance, a speck appeared.

::Fear not. Afran is a friend, and his kin, Karis, rides on his back.::

Jae stared at the black speck off in the distance. She could see no rider, but the dragon was tiny yet.

Spluttering laughter. ::He is not tiny—in fact, he is rather large. But he is calm and wise, and the other dragons listen to him.::

::He was also the only one willing to spend hours in the cold sky this morning,:: said a dry voice Jae didn't recognize. ::I'm Karis, youngling, and I'm delighted to meet you. We'll have you tucked into some warm soup in a short while.::

Jae knew she was hungry. She could feel the weakness in her wings. But it was a small thing. She was flying. In the light. With three others in the huge sky, even if two were still far away—and she could feel their sincerity and their honest, open warmth.

They looked on her wings and saw nothing to fear.

Choking sadness tangled with the joy inside her. This had been missing her entire life.

::It is not missing any longer.:: Fendellen sounded gentle and terribly fierce. ::There will be those who will not accept, but they do not live in the village. And no dragon will shun you. This, I promise.::

Jae blinked at the certainty in Fendellen's voice. And then blinked again because the much larger dragon was getting closer, and he was as big as a mountain. She could feel her wings trembling. If he decided she was to be feared, no one would be able to say differently.

Spluttering from the dragon beside her—and then an

odd silence.

One that might have worried Jae more if the enormous black dragon hadn't turned neatly in the sky in a way she would have found challenging with her much smaller body, and lined up with her wing tip. The woman on his back held up a small bag. "If I throw this, can you catch? There are two meat pies inside. I don't expect they're very warm anymore, but they will fill the gaping hole in your belly until we can get more food in you."

She was flying in the sky with dragons, and they were talking about food.

Jae felt like she'd flown headfirst into an enormous tree, but she managed to get her hands on the small satchel that was thrown her way. Gran was fond of tossing things, and woe to the apprentice who dropped a medicine that had taken days or weeks to make.

She wasn't sure her belly even remembered how to be hungry anymore, but one careful look in the satchel proved she was wrong. There were indeed two meat pies nestled in a cloth inside the well-used leather, and one sniff had her mouth watering so much, she nearly drooled.

::Slowly, youngling.:: Karis, somehow still talking in her head. ::If you've not eaten for a while, just a bite or two until we see if your belly is going to rebel.::

Jae could have pointed out that even the lowliest healer's apprentice never forgot that lesson after they'd worn the consequences a time or two, but she was too busy breaking off a bite and trying to hold the satchel close enough to her mouth that she didn't lose a single bit of the flaky pastry.

::There's a whole tray of them waiting when you get to

the village.:: Afran this time, and he sounded amused. ::Kellan knows how much Fendellen likes them.::

Shame flamed in Jae's cheeks. She turned upside down and came up just below her dragon, flying belly to belly, and held up the satchel. ::I didn't know they were to share. I'm so sorry.::

::They're not, sweet one. I ate before I flew last night, so my stomach can wait for Kellan's tray.:: Fendellen's eyes were wide with surprise. ::But that's a very impressive flying trick.::

Jae ducked out of her dragon's way and resumed a more sedate flight beside her. ::I'm sorry. I wasn't trying to show off.::

She didn't miss the exchange of glances across her wings. Or the flash of anger in Fendellen's eyes, but it was the dark dragon who spoke. ::Youngling, I believe you'll discover that dragons appreciate talented flying—and it appears you are well matched. Fendellen is one of our most skilled fliers.::

The idea that she might be a *good* flier was so far beyond Jae's ken that she could hardly find her words. ::The eagles are far better than I am.::

She heard Karis's bright laugh, outside her head this time instead of inside it. ::That's a high standard you have. I only know of one or two dragons who could have pulled off that upside-down maneuver close in like you just did, and I get the feeling you weren't even trying hard.::

Jae had no idea what to say. Absolutely none at all.

But as she flew over the bright snow, flanked by two dragons, something inside her that had been twisted and tight for as long as she could remember started to loosen.

INTERLUDE

Lovissa felt her tail thump in the snow of the ledge she had landed on, and sighed. She knew better than to let her discomfort reveal itself in her body. Such things could get a dragon warrior filled with arrows.

She used her tail to brush more of the snow from the flat rock instead. One of her favorite thinking places in summer, but in the dead of winter, her attendants would have fits that she had left the warmth of cave and home.

They didn't understand a queen's need for solitude.

She had much to think about. The Dragon Star had marked the fourth pair, and only five were needed. Her dragons might be spending the winter in rare relaxation, but Lovissa could feel the weight of prophecy descending from the sky.

A weight an ice-blue dragon was trying to pull onto her own scales and not share.

Lovissa blew smoke and fire out into the chill air. She shouldn't doubt the choices of one who would be queen, but this troubled her. *The star had called the girl. Firmly and clearly and with some recklessness. Lovissa knew little of humans, but that one had been near dead with cold before Fendellen had shown up.*

It wasn't for queens to question stars, either, but she was out here on this ledge because her opinions, sharp and discontented, refused to quiet.

Perhaps the Dragon Star had reasons for its haste. And if it did, Fendellen's choice might bring disaster to the dragons of the Veld.

Lovissa knew, all too well, the necessity of time—and its dangerous allure. She yearned for it. Time for her dragons to live. To dance and write ballads and eat too much. They kept watch on the passes still, but they saw elves only rarely. And two more clans had presented Timot with broken dragonkiller arrows. That wasn't nearly all of them, even on the northern slopes. But it was momentous, even so.

Or a softening of her warriors that might hasten their end.

She blew out a stream of fire over a small valley that would be lovely in spring, refusing to let her tail thump like an agitated youngster.

There were good reasons not to fight. Strong ones. Ones that would make time for Quira to grow, and their next generation of warriors. Too much pressure too young, and even those with the finest hearts and minds could crack. It had happened all too often when the battles did not wait for their fighters to be ready.

There were no signs of battle. No portents of impending doom.

Save for one. The prophecy spoke of the five who would save dragonkind. Surely they did not come to save her dragons from badly rhymed ballads and bellies overfilled with food.

Which meant this lull, this tranquility, this peace—would not last.

Lovissa blew fire again, a queen's futile response to dreams that came with muddled messages and far too few answers. And sent a thought she knew Fendellen would never hear. ::Don't wait too long.::

PART II
FRIENDS & FEATHERS

CHAPTER 8

*J*ae set down her empty mug of broth and gulped. She'd been treated so very kindly. They'd landed right beside a huge, strange round hut, and she'd been hurried in to a place by the fire, wrapped in blankets, and plied with fluffy bread and tasty broth. Karis peeked in on her every so often, but otherwise, she had been left alone.

Which must be Fendellen's doing. Jae hadn't been brave enough to wish for solitude out loud.

::It was, sweet one. Are you ready to come out?::

Jae gulped again, but her belly was full now, and there were no longer any excuses to keep hiding. None that Gran would have accepted, anyhow, and repaying kindness with cowardice went against everything Jae had ever been taught. She held on to the edge of the table and stood, giving herself a moment to find her balance. It was an odd sensation to stand and walk with her wings unbound.

She reached for the large cloak hanging on a peg by the

kitchen door. Karis had left it for her after taking a good look at Jae's boots and deciding they were acceptable. The cloak was almost as thick as the ones of the high mountains, and she wrapped herself in its comforting scratchy weight. Then she swallowed, because it was far shorter than the one she'd left behind. It did very little to hide her wings.

She felt the need to scurry into hiding like a little mouse clawing at her belly. She'd caught only glimpses of the village as they had landed, but it was far bigger than home and full of strangeness. Round houses and paths far wider than any human would need, and scattered bits and pieces lying around that would blow away in the high mountains.

There must be so many people living in those houses. More than she could count on all her fingers and toes and probably Fendellen's claws, too. Maybe even more than when the traveling markets came to the mountains and people journeyed in from days around.

A head popped in the door of the kitchen, and an icy wind with it. Fendellen's eyes scanned her top to bottom. ::That should keep you warm enough for a bit.::

Jae wasn't worried about being cold, although after five days of worrying about little else, perhaps she should take more care. ::My village is small. This one is very large. Are there many people outside?:: Wanting a glimpse of the newcomer, no doubt.

Fendellen winced. ::More than a few. And quite a number of dragons as well.::

Of course. Both lived here, although that was even

harder to imagine than round houses and a village bigger than a market festival.

::Come. Karis is clearing a rondo for us, so we'll be tucked away soon enough, but a new kin bond doesn't happen very often, and you've hidden in the kitchen long enough.::

That briskness that reminded her so much of Gran. Jae straightened her shoulders. The villagers weren't waiting to stare at her wings. They were waiting to stare at her dragon, or at least at the two of them together, and she didn't want to embarrass the beautiful flying creature that had somehow chosen her.

Fendellen snorted. ::We were chosen for each other. This is as much your fault as mine, youngling.::

The oddness of that thought accompanied Jae out the door. She took a deep breath of the bracing air. It was warmer than home, and far less windy, but winter nonetheless. She tipped her head to the sky, checking for any sign of the sun behind the clouds, an instinct well honed in any child of the mountains.

"It's about halfway between midday and nightfall," Karis said cheerfully, stepping in to her side. "We've cleared out a rondo for you to sleep in." She gestured at one of the strange round huts. "It's got a small bed and lots of blankets. If that doesn't suit you, we can see what else we can wrangle."

Jae stared. A whole family could live in the very smallest of the round houses. And an entire bed to herself was vast and strange.

"Families share beds in the mountains. I imagine she'll find a bed of her own plenty suitable." The older man who stepped in to her other side was gruff and fierce, but his eyes were kind. "I'm Irin. I'll be the one teaching you to use a weapon properly once the spring melts come, but until then, I'm busy in the nursery. I'm kin bonded to Kis. He would like to hear the stories of your home when you have time to tell them. It's a long while since we visited the mountains. The skies there were good flying."

He knew something of the mountains. Jae let that settle some of the tightness trying to curdle the broth in her belly.

A peach-pink head ducked around his arm and nearly licked Jae's nose.

Fendellen rumbled, and Irin glared, but it was the look one would give to a misbehaving child. "This trouble-maker is Lotus. She's kin to Sapphire, who should be around here somewhere."

"Here," said a voice that sounded very short of breath. "Karis said we were to stay out of sight until Jae was ready to meet us. I listened. Lotus clearly forgot where she put her ears this morning."

Jae stared at the small elf with hair the color of burnished straw and dark, vivid eyes that told stories even when she wasn't saying a word. She gulped and held out both hands in the way of the mountains. "I'm Jae, and I'm pleased to meet you." That wasn't entirely true, but it was the polite thing to say, and maybe if she worked hard enough to believe it, it would become true.

Sapphire's eyes lit with pleasure as more people suddenly crowded around. "These are my friends, Lily and Alonia and Kellan."

Jae could feel her head trying to explode. Four young

women her own age in one village? She blinked, panic knocking against the backs of her knees.

"Your dress is beautiful. You'll have to show me how you make those stitches."

"Are you still hungry?"

"Fendellen is a wonderful dragon. Where did she find you?"

Jae didn't know which ones had spoken. She was too busy watching the elf with dark hair and the dragon that had poked its head up the back of her cloak.

The elf reached under her cloak, a wry look on her face. "This is Oceana. She hates winter and loves climbing me like I'm a tree."

Mellie's little boy was like that.

Mellie.

Something crashed inside Jae's head like a pile of drying pots and pans that had gotten too tall and finally fallen over. Mellie was five days away, and so were Gran and home and everything she had ever known. This strange place was full of too many questions and too many eyes peeking out of doors and around buildings and walking down the wide paths of the village like this many people was something that happened every day.

She tried to breathe in, but the only way the air wanted to go was out, like when she was small and Rubia pulled the goat's tail and it kicked Jae instead. She put her hands to her ribs, trying to make them work, trying to get her throat to let the chill air in.

Small black flecks swirled in front of her eyes.

Scared faces.

She felt the deep concern inside her head from her dragon.

And then only darkness.

~

Fendellen licked up the last vestiges of a most delicious bowl of stew. She could feel the drafts as people came and went from the rondo. Checking on Jae. Refreshing straw that was perfectly fine just the way it was. Bringing small pretties and special treats and other things humans and dragons tried to use to apologize for wrongness when they didn't truly understand what had gone wrong.

Fendellen understood. She had been attached to Jae's mind when it went dark.

"That's enough fretting, missy."

Irin picked up her bowl and handed it out to someone she couldn't quite see.

Fendellen gave him a look. Very few invaded a dragon's sleeping nook, especially when that dragon would one day be queen.

He slid down a wall onto a pile of soft straw and returned her look. "Karis is chasing everyone out. I didn't want to disturb your kin, so we'll talk in here. I know how you whine when you have to go outside in the cold."

His words loosened the tightness inside her a little. "I was barely hatched, and it was my first winter." She'd thrown an unholy tantrum when her feet hit the snow, which had earned her not a whit of sympathy from man or dragon.

"Indeed." A pause. "New experiences can be over-whelming."

They weren't talking about snow anymore. "I can't see everything in her mind clearly, but I think the village she was raised in is tiny."

"They all are that high up." Irin shrugged. "A few families and the orphans they take in."

That was a disturbing thought. "There are a lot of orphans?"

"The mountains are a dangerous place. And villagers from the foothills often leave unwanted babies close to one of the high-mountain villages."

Fendellen shuddered. There were some things about humans she would never understand. Rejecting their young was one of the foremost. "Jae was left to die. She knows it. It weakens her, somewhere deep inside."

"Then we help her become strong."

He was so solid. So certain. She leaned into his strength, even though a future queen should rely on her own. "She isn't as fragile as today made her look."

He was quiet for a long time. "I've seen what happened to her in others. Panic that grips the throat and doesn't let it breathe. It hits some soldiers in their first battle. For some, it's less serious than it looks, and it doesn't happen again. For others, it's their last battle."

There was more than one possible reason for that, and none of them were good. She shuddered to think of a sword run through Jae's ribs as she stood frozen by fear. "This isn't a battle. We have time."

A steady look—one that wasn't altogether approving. "You have a *little* time."

She had more than that. The humans and elves and dragons of the village had been warned, and they knew better than to face a future queen's fury.

"It's a complicated choice you made."

A man who never let anything rest. Fire rose in Fendellen's belly. "The sight of a crowded village knocked her out cold, and you think I should tell her anything more?"

She was careful in her words. Even in sleep, Jae might hear.

"She isn't as fragile as today made her look."

Fendellen grimaced as the weapons master tossed her own words back at her. "She isn't. She flew for five days with very little food, following the call of some cursed star. She might lack for common sense, but she doesn't lack for determination."

Another long pause as Irin carefully plucked several bits of straw and lined them up in his fingers. "Karis says she expects to be shunned for her wings."

The fire hadn't entirely settled. "Anyone who tries will deal with me."

"You know better than that."

There were a lot of ways he could mean that, and she didn't have the energy to play dueling word swords with a master. "I know she's had a very long day and tomorrow is a new one." She swallowed her pride because sometimes a queen had to know how to do that too. "She needs to feel accepted. If you have ideas about how to accomplish that, I would like to hear them."

He huffed out something that might be a laugh in anyone else.

She waited. She meant it, and under his gruffness, he

knew well just how much of her respect he commanded. And she wanted his help. He knew how to straighten spines and snap shoulders into place, and her kin needed both of those things.

He set down his neatly straightened handful of straw. "I have an idea or two."

CHAPTER 9

*I*t was a bed so soft she might be sleeping on clouds, except she remembered enough of yesterday to be quite sure she wasn't dead.

Jae opened up her eyes as more memories flooded in. There had been eyes, so many eyes and faces—and then nothing.

"Good morning." The voice from the door was friendly, and attached to a smiling face and a tray that immediately set Jae's belly to growling. "If you're hungry, I have breakfast for you."

Jae dug for a name. Kellan. "Thank you. I'm very sorry about yesterday. I don't quite remember what happened."

"What happened," said a new voice from the door, this one with more than a hint of Gran's acerbic tones, "is that half the village tried to get a look at you all at once, and you did the same thing my dragon does. You shut down for a while and had a nap."

That elf walked in with two more on her heels. The

four of them took off their boots and cloaks, chattering quietly with each other and demanding nothing of Jae, and sat down on the second bed in the room. They didn't stare at her. They just made themselves comfortable and helped themselves to food from Kellan's tray.

Jae swallowed. She had dreamed her whole life of friends her own age. Ones who saw a person before they saw her wings. If she could keep her head on her shoulders, maybe this was her chance. "Do you all have dragons?"

The fair-haired one with round cheeks looked up from spreading some kind of jelly on her bread. "Kellan doesn't yet. She rides Afran sometimes, though. The rest of us are kin. I'm the newest. Trift only found me this past summer."

"She's Alonia." The dark-haired elf poured something hot out of a carafe into mugs. "I'm Lily, and my dragon is Oceana. She's the small blue creature who was climbing under my cloak yesterday. That's Sapphire over there on the end. Her dragon is Lotus, and she's in trouble more often than not."

Jae collected the names like precious jewels.

Alonia held out a slice of bread covered in a thick spread of jelly. "There's cheese, if you'd rather."

Goat cheese was a winter staple in the high mountains, but anything made of berries was a wonderful treat. Jae took the bread carefully.

Sapphire grinned and layered cheese between two slices of bread. "So, what's it like being able to fly?"

Alonia made shushing noises, and Kellan frowned.

Lily rolled her eyes. "The grownups think we should be gentle with you and not talk about anything important for a while."

Jae's hands shook, and the jelly along with it. "I don't mind questions. It's just that no one ever asks about my wings." They just stared, and judged, and sometimes hated. She saw none of that in these four. They only ate bread with jelly and watched her with friendly curiosity in their eyes. She took a deep breath. "I fly at night so I don't scare anyone. In winter, the stars are so bright, I feel like I can touch them."

Kellan smiled, a dreamy look in her eyes. "That would be amazing. And cold."

Jae shrugged. "I grew up in the high mountains. I'm used to cold."

Lily shuddered. "I like it warm, thank you very much." She dipped a spoon in the jelly pot and plopped a big dollop on a new slice of bread. "I heard that Fendellen made you a hot pool in the cave you stayed in. If you liked that, you should come swim in my pool."

The idea that anyone had such a pool for their very own stole Jae's breath. She curled her wings around herself, trying to imagine such a wonder—and then froze as four sets of eyes got wide.

She reached for the covers. If she wrapped them around her shoulders, maybe that would hide her wings until she could find her cloak. Or make a new one—one that hung all the way to the ground this time.

"They're beautiful." Kellan's words were quiet. "Your wings. They're so pretty." She held out a hesitant hand. "Could I touch your feathers?"

Jae stared. None but the very littlest ever wanted to touch. She lifted a wing tip and tried to breathe.

Kellan touched. A single finger at first, and then a tiny

sound of delight as she stroked with her whole hand. "Oh. They're so soft."

The softest ones were underneath, but Jae was too overwhelmed to form the words.

Alonia scooted a little closer. "Do your feathers ever come out?"

Jae managed a nod. "Sometimes."

"I like to do fancy stitching." Alonia looked a little shy. "I'd like to try copying a feather, if I could borrow one for a while. Or I could use the small ones for decoration."

Gran had always told her to leave any she lost out in the forest. "You can have as many as you like."

Lily shook her head as Alonia bounced gleefully and Sapphire chased the bread that was trying to fall jelly-side down on the floor. "You'll knock us all off the bed, silly. Or cover us in jelly."

Jae could feel the tears trying to come again.

This kind of closeness and easy conversation and playful silliness existed in her village too. She just never got to sit and feel a part of it.

Alonia grinned from her spot in the middle of the bed. "I can do normal sewing too. Would you like some help altering that cloak you were wearing yesterday so it doesn't cover up your wings? That must have been really uncomfortable."

Jae stared, her speech gone again.

Alonia's head dipped, her cheeks turning red. "I'm sorry. That wasn't a nice thing to say."

"No." The single word spilled out before Jae could think. "It's not that. I've always covered my wings. In my village, I wrapped them tight to my body to hide them."

Lily wrinkled her nose. "Then how could you fly?"

"She didn't," Kellan said quietly, watching Jae's face. "Only at night when no one could see you, right?"

Jae nodded.

"My clan wasn't always nice to people who were different." Sapphire glanced at Jae and then looked down at her knees. "I had a cousin who couldn't say all the words right, and sometimes the others would tease him. I bet it was even worse with wings."

They were trying to understand. "People are sometimes scared of what they don't know." It was something Gran said often, even if it was little comfort to a sore heart.

Lily snorted. "People are sometimes idiots. It's good that you're here now."

So many faces. They couldn't possibly all be this friendly. "I don't want to scare anyone here."

Lily gave her a look like the one Gran used when she was trying to figure out which remedy would best help a patient. "When I first brought Oceana here, she was really cranky. She wasn't used to people and she hated fire, and none of the other dragons were sure what to do with her."

Jae understood the lesson behind the words. "I'll try not to be cranky."

All of them laughed. Alonia elbowed Lily. "Too bad. You'll still be the crankiest of us all."

Lily made a face. "Whatever."

Sapphire grinned and stole Lily's bread. "What she's trying to say is you're not the first person or dragon to arrive in this village who's a little different."

Wings weren't little. Jae looked helplessly at the feathers taking up half her bed.

Sapphire sobered. "We all have things that make us different. Lily can't cook and her dragon doesn't like fire, which is really strange for a dragon. Lotus and I were too scared to fly and Trift still won't, and he does magic with Alonia, which is even stranger than not liking fire."

Jae felt dizzy, like her head had a spinning hoop inside it. "Magic?"

"Yup." Alonia sighed and made a face. "The first thing we did was turn the weapons master's sword into a flower, so trust me, anyone who might be worried about a few feathers left this village a long time ago."

It had never occurred to Jae that there might be a place where she wasn't the most frightening inhabitant. And even magic probably wasn't as scary as fire-breathing dragons. She felt the lightness of that thought lifting her wings—but it wasn't until Kellan grinned that she realized she was smiling.

She took a breath and let it get bigger.

Four faces beamed back at her.

Kellan nodded. "I think you'll be a good kin for Fend-ellen. Karis says you're already a really amazing flier, but you'll know how to be her friend, too."

Jae didn't miss the slightly strained looks that passed between her new friends, but she wasn't going to let anything dampen her happiness. Gran said that if you opened your mind, the plants would teach you in their own time. She would let this village teach her too. "You all did so much for me yesterday. What work can I do?"

Lily rolled her eyes. "Don't worry about that. Work will come find you, and we can show you all the good hiding spots for when there's too much of it."

Jae ducked her head and smiled. Lily sounded like Mellie. Good-natured complaining from someone who never actually shirked her work.

"We need to find you some clothes." Alonia brushed a few crumbs off her knees. "I have two dresses that are a bit small for me, so we can start with those. Or we can make you some tunics, like Kellan wears."

No girl old enough to walk wore anything but a dress in the high mountains, but Kellan's leggings looked warm and practical, especially for a healer's apprentice. And skirts were neither warm nor practical to fly in.

"Right. Tunics, then." Alonia grinned. "I'll go talk to Inga. I think she still has some bolts of wool from the fall fair, and there are probably some pants and long shirts in the storage bins that we can tuck and alter a bit. Lily can help with the basic sewing, and then you can show me how to do the fancy stitching on your dress and we can copy it to your tunics."

"I don't mind sewing," Jae said quietly. "I'm sure you all have your own work to do."

Sapphire shrugged. "We do, but you can help with some of that too. Tomorrow we'll go play with the babies so Irin doesn't yell."

That steadied Jae. She knew how to mind littles.

Kellan popped up and set mugs and crumbs and bits of leftover cheese back on the tray. "I'll get us some food for while we sew." She smiled at Jae. "I'm a terrible seamstress, but Alonia won't let me wreck your clothes. Are there things you particularly like to eat?"

Jae had no idea how to answer that. "Anything that fills my belly."

Kellan laughed and carried the tray over to her cloak and boots. "That I can promise to deliver."

Alonia lined up behind her. "I'll go raid the storage bins and Inga's woolens." She gave Jae a cheery wink. "I think your dragon is waiting to say good morning, but don't go far. It's nice and warm in here, so we'll spend the day here, if that's all right."

Jae nodded, dazed.

A day spent hiding with new friends sounded far more than just all right.

CHAPTER 10

*T*he littles weren't human.
They were *dragons*.

Jae stared at the three tiny creatures currently sitting up and staring back at her and tried not to turn into spring-melt at their cuteness.

Irin chuckled. "Don't let them fool you. They're just as much trouble as full-grown dragons, and far less likely to clean up their own messes." He picked up a well-worn leather bag at the door to the nursery. "Karis will be within earshot, and Afran will know where to find me."

Sapphire rolled her eyes, but Jae noticed she didn't do it where the gruff older man could see.

Kellan nodded respectfully. "We'll be fine. We'll take good care of them, and we promise to listen to Kis."

A large golden eye opened on the far side of the nursery, and Jae jumped backwards—straight into Fendellen behind her.

::Easy, sweet one. He's large and grumpy, and his kindness knows no bounds. He's also hurting this morning. He carries many old wounds of war, and the winter cold makes all his aches and pains worse.::

Jae kept her eyes on the yellow scales of a dragon who looked almost as big as Afran. ::Can your healers not help him?::

::It's rare for a dragon to suffer grievous injury. Elf healers do what they can. His kin has searched lands far and wide for things that will help him.::

Then a high-mountain healer's apprentice would know nothing that hadn't already been tried. She dipped her head respectfully. ::I'm sorry he hurts.::

The eye closed slightly, as if it had heard her.

"This is Squirt." Sapphire was already sitting on the floor, a tiny purple dragon baby in her lap nibbling something from her fingers. "That's her nickname, anyhow, until the queen or her kin finds her real one. She's the smallest of the three, but she's always hungry."

Jae tried to gather her wits. "Sometimes the smallest ones need to eat to catch up."

Kellan giggled. "I've been trying that forever and it hasn't worked yet."

Fendellen made her way carefully over to a space near Kis. "I'll lie down over here, and you can lean against me and protect me from their fierce little claws."

Jae was pretty sure her dragon didn't need protecting from anything much, but a safe place to sit and watch was very welcome. She took a step Fendellen's way and then froze as the baby the same color as Kis finally lifted her face out of Kellan's bowl. Her head was oddly shaped, like a rock had landed on her egg and squished it, and she had only knobs where her short front legs should be.

Jae heard a sound, sharp and sad, and realized it was her own.

A moment later, there was a sound in reply. A hiss, from the largest of the babies, this one black and on his feet in front of the yellow baby.

Jae dropped to her knees, making herself smaller. Less scary. "I would not hurt her. Not ever. This I promise." Her heart beat fast and full of aches. No one but Gran had ever protected her so fiercely. "You are a good friend."

Fendellen lowered her nose to the small black one. "This is Taenin."

Jae gave him a nod of respect and then held out her hand, very carefully, to the small yellow dragon. "Do you like to be scratched, little one? My wings get awfully itchy sometimes in places I can't reach."

Bright gold eyes stared at her fingers.

Jae didn't move. "There are flowers growing near my village that are the same color as your scales. They're called amarilli, and they're very brave, one of the first to poke their heads up through the snow in spring." She gulped, but said the next thought anyhow. "Sometimes there is another snowfall and the flowers end up looking a little squished. My gran taught me that those are the most special flowers. We never pick them because they give strong medicine back to the mountain."

A small golden head tilted, and then trilled, high and sharp and surprisingly loud.

Fendellen rumbled in reply. "You like that name, do

you, little one? We could call you Rilli." She nodded at Jae. "It suits her. A good name for a special dragon."

A small head rubbing against her fingers seemed to agree.

It was a good name. A strong name. Perhaps it would help keep her safe in a world that didn't always tolerate differences very well.

::The world of humans and elves, perhaps.:: There was disdain in the ice-blue dragon's tone. And anger. ::Dragons know to appreciate the gift of the special ones. Their strong medicine is not meant only for mountains.::

Jae stared—and then felt the sharp tug on the lacings of the pants they'd altered yesterday. A small black dragon seemed rather astonished that they were still attached to her, and gave another pull.

Kellan giggled. "Nothing is safe from these three."

Jae reached down and gently disengaged her clothes. These were her only pants for now, and they were so much more comfortable than a long woolen skirt. She scratched Taenin's head and looked up at the older man who ran the nursery and had somehow not yet made it out the door. "Do you have any old leather lacings? In my village, we made ones with knots for babies to chew on."

Irin inclined his head slightly and reached for a basket tucked up on a high shelf. "I have some remnants from binding knife handles."

Rilli butted her head up against Jae's other hand, clearly wanting some of what Taenin was getting.

Jae smiled. They weren't so very different from the littles of home.

Kellan moved closer to help with the scratching and laughed as Rilli backed up into her strong fingers.

Jae watched. "Are dragons always so itchy?"

"The littles are." Irin handed down some lengths of leather lacing. "They grow fast at this stage, and scales don't adjust quite as easily as human skin."

"They're twice as big as when they hatched." Kellan sounded as proud as if she'd laid every egg herself. She shook her head fondly at Rilli. "Only silly dragons pick midwinter to come into the world, though."

Sapphire snorted, disentangling a purple dragon from her hair. "At least they didn't decide to hatch up in a tree." She rolled her eyes at Jae. "That's where I found Lotus."

That sounded scary even for someone with wings, and Sapphire didn't have any. And it sounded sad. Jae knew all too well why some newly born babies ended up in scary places. "Did her mother not want her?"

Sapphire winced, her face full of guilt.

Fendellen whiffed softly at Sapphire's blonde hair. "We don't know. Dragon young are cared for by all, but eggs are usually left safely in the hatching forest."

Jae smiled down at her knees and the two tiny dragons curling up there together. Maybe humans needed hatching forests too. "Gran found me on the side of a mountain." She tipped her head back up and met Sapphire's eyes. Dragon babies high in trees weren't any more likely to survive than newborn babes on exposed mountainsides. "I'm glad you found Lotus."

Sapphire grinned. "The first time she barrel rolls through the village and lands you headfirst in a water trough, remember you said that."

The others laughed, but it was rueful enough that obviously such things had been known to happen. Jae shifted a little, making her lap more comfortable for the two who had chosen to nap there. Then she picked the leather lacing back up to continue her knotting.

Irin glanced at the small project. "You're used to having busy hands."

Always. She'd heard tales of idle hands in the lowlands, but no one from a high mountain village truly believed them, and healers were kept busier than most. "There were always clothes to mend or medicines to make or leather to soften."

He nodded approvingly.

"You sew as well as Alonia does." Sapphire sounded impressed.

Jae hid a smile. Sapphire's sewing skills weren't much better than a little's. "The high mountains are hard on clothes, and if I wanted any to wear, I had to rework Mellie's cast-offs."

Kellan raised a silent eyebrow in question.

"She was Gran's other apprentice." Jae smiled and hoped her words didn't sound too sad. "She has a little boy. He wasn't old enough to be scared of me yet. I spent time with him most afternoons." Soaking in the easy acceptance. Readying for the day when he would look at her with careful eyes.

From the look in Kellan's eyes, she'd clearly picked up on the sadness. "Did you have wings when your gran found you?"

Jae nodded and looked down at the two sleeping littles

in her lap. "Yes, but small creatures are always sweet, no matter how scary they might be when they grow up."

"Indeed," Fendellen said dryly, shooting a glance at Kis.

Jae was pretty sure she would find both Irin and Kis frightening under other circumstances, but clearly, they didn't feel the same way about her. The women of the village had let Jae tend to their babies, but most of them only under Gran's watchful eye. There were eyes watching here, but they felt different. Felt like, just maybe, they saw her, and not just the strange appendages she had been born with.

It was terrifying to hope, but as she watched a yellow belly rise and fall in her lap, she wanted very much to believe that this place might have enough room for a girl with feathers and a dragon with a squished head to spread their wings.

CHAPTER 11

*J*ae gulped. She had walked the whole way to the kitchen with her feathers showing. All of them. Alonia had helped her alter the shoulders and neck of her cloak to fit snugly, but not hamper her wings. Which had seemed daring enough in the safe confines of her rondo. Out here, the courage required for each step had nearly stolen her breath.

She reached for the door of the much larger rondo where most of the cooking happened. Perhaps she could hide a while and make herself useful.

A face popped out the door before she could head inside. "Hullo. You must be Jae." The older woman eyed her up and down like she might be for sale on the next market day. "You look level-headed enough."

Jae nodded, a little dazed. This could only be Inga, and if the stories she'd heard so far were true, this was Inga at her most cheerful.

The other woman nodded briskly. "There's snow up on

the roof. I was waiting for Afran to come take care of it, but word is, he's too busy this morning to deal with minor matters." Her tone said precisely what she thought about this being considered a minor matter. She stepped farther out the door and held out a stiff broom. "This ought to do the trick. Send the snow down the back, if you please, and not onto my kitchen herbs."

Jae blinked, and then blinked again because the first time hadn't improved her comprehension any. "I'm sorry. I don't understand what you want me to do."

Inga gave her a look that said she had precious little tolerance for addleheaded helpers. "I want you to fly up and knock the snow off the roof. It sits on the flat part at the top, and then the fire warms it during the day and it freezes back up overnight. I get holes in my roof that way, and you get bits of roof in your bread." She held out the broom again, twitching it upward. "Go on then. It won't take you but a minute, and I bet you're a lot more useful with a broom than any dragon."

Jae stared at the broom. And then at Inga. And then up at the roof, which sure enough did have an island of snow sitting on the flattest part of the dome. It was the reason mountain huts had steeply pitched roofs, but those would have to be awfully high to fit dragons.

Slowly, feeling caught in an avalanche and unable to move fast enough to break free, she took the broom. She shook out her feathers a little, which Inga watched with about as much curiosity as a rising loaf of bread.

No one here had looked at her with fear in their eyes.

Jae took a deep breath and flapped just hard enough to lift her feet off the ground. Inga's eyes widened a little, but she flicked her fingers impatiently. "Go, youngling. I've soup to tend, and then I need my broom back."

Something almost like a giggle tried to sneak out, but Jae swallowed it back. She lifted farther off the ground, at an angle so she didn't flap air at Inga's dress and hair. When she reached the height of the snowpack, she looked around, orienting herself. It wouldn't do to send snow onto the garden, or onto Inga's head, either. She picked a direction that seemed equipped for a small influx of snow and swept the broom gingerly.

A snort from below had her nearly dropping it.

Karis shook her head, a hand shading her eyes. "You'll want something different than a broom, I'm thinking."

Inga glared at her. "The dragons manage with a broom."

"The dragons have claws to break things up." Karis looked roofward again. "Afran says that what's up there is more ice than snow."

Jae could see that with her own eyes now. Her cheeks flushed. Even a small child from the high mountains would know better than to try to sweep an ice pack. She turned the broom over. It had a good, sturdy handle. She studied the drift lines in the compacted snow and the gentle sloping of the roof. Then she drilled the handle into the snow. Once, twice, and on the third time, a large chunk broke off and headed for the ground.

"There." Inga sounded pleased. "A broom will work just fine. And a youngling with some common sense is a welcome addition to this village."

"Indeed she is." Karis sounded like she was trying very hard not to laugh.

"Bring my broom back when you're finished." Inga nodded crisply and disappeared from sight.

Jae stared down at Karis, bemused and bewildered. Chores were nothing new, and she was happy to do them, but Inga was acting for all the world like a human with wings was handy and nothing more.

Footsteps sounded in the crunchy snow, and a woman she didn't know came around the corner, dusting off her shoulders and cursing imaginatively. She glanced at Karis and then up at the roof.

Jae froze.

The woman's face brightened. "Well now, aren't you a sight for sore eyes? I don't suppose you might have a moment when you're done with that? I'm Ana, wagon master for the village. I've got a sled we're trying to dig out of a snowbank, and I need a good angle on a rope. We've got a boulder to wrap around, but someone with wings and hands would surely be useful. Claws aren't much good for tying knots in ropes."

Somehow, Jae managed to get her mouth closed. She nodded, at a loss for words, and held up her broom.

Ana nodded cheerfully. "When you're done with that, then. I'll go see if I can get some warm cider for the both of us while I wait."

Jae watched, dazed, as Ana disappeared through the door into the kitchen.

Karis chuckled. "I suspect people will find enough good uses for someone with wings and hands that you might need to make it clear that you still need to eat and sleep."

She didn't mind hard work. It was the idea that her

wings were useful that was draining all the sense from Jae's head. She shook it to kick the cobwebs loose and thunked the broom end into the snow again. A variation of a chore she'd done so many times that it didn't bear thinking about—but always, her wings had been hidden. Bound.

She stretched them a little farther under the weak winter sun.

She was flying. In daylight. Where people could see.

More crunching footsteps down below, these ones fast. Jae looked down, startled to see Irin charging away from the nursery.

Karis spun around and nearly got her head clipped by a tiny purple flying menace—a purple menace wobbling like the last man leaving the pub on midwinter's night.

Jae didn't remember her first flights, but Gran had stories, ones that involved big lumps on the head of a small girl. She pulled in her wings enough to maneuver easily and eased her way toward Squirt. The baby dragon was climbing, which made sense—it was the easiest direction to go when you had no idea how your wings worked. Unfortunately, it had also put her out of reach of the two people on the ground.

Irin nodded his head sharply. "She's never done this before. The dragons are coming, but whatever safety you can provide…"

That was all Jae needed to hear.

::We're on our way, sweet one.:: Fendellen sounded worried. ::The air currents in the village can be tricky.::

Especially in winter. Heat and cold. Nothing to faze a larger, heavier flier, but Squirt was so very tiny. Jae did her best to hover between Squirt and the ground, not at all sure she could catch the baby dragon if she fell.

The small flier flapped mightily, making up in determination what she lacked in wing span and coordination. And then a rogue updraft caught her, spinning her nearly around.

Jae scooted in closer, heart in her throat, ready to try plucking a baby dragon out of the sky and taking her to safety.

Until she looked into two dark eyes. Ones that held no fear, no caution. Only pure, exhilarated joy.

It wasn't in Jae to take that away. She had lived her whole life steeped in fear and caution, and she would not be the one who taught Squirt the harder ways of the world. She flipped over onto her back, just like she had done with Fendellen, carefully adjusting her own flight until she was belly to belly with the small dragon, less than two hands of space between them.

Squirt's eyes beamed surprise and delight. Her little wings stretched out, riding the calmer air.

::We're here.::

Jae felt the small drafts as an ice-blue dragon came alongside them, and then, with barely a shifting in the air at all, Afran's enormous presence on the other side. His enormous dark eye watched her calmly. ::We will make sure you don't run into any trees.::

She blinked. ::We should keep flying?::

Fendellen's laughter bubbled in her head. ::She's safe now, and we would no more dim her joy than you would.::

The small purple head turned gingerly, eyeing the

dragons on either side of her. Then she raised her head proudly and flapped fiercely. Moving faster. Climbing.

::Younglings.:: Afran sounded amused. ::Challenging us to a race already, she is.::

::She'll learn soon enough that you're a lot faster than you look.::

That didn't surprise Jae at all. She could tell just how skilled a flier he was by how little he disturbed the air with his bulk. Jae realized he was doing more than just flying steady—he was also blocking the troublesome currents, keeping the air flows under her smooth just as she was doing for Squirt. She angled slightly, taking better advantage of the flows he made.

::Do you tire?:: Fendellen sounded worried again.

Jae looked at Squirt's excited eyes. ::No.::

A fond chuckle. ::Liar.::

Jae felt her cheeks warm. ::It's a little awkward to fly this way, but nothing I can't do for a while longer. She'll tire soon enough.::

::Indeed.:: Afran's voice was wry. ::She shouldn't be in the sky for months yet. Irin will be fit to be tied.::

::Not much escapes his nursery.:: Fendellen's tones were fond. ::It's good to keep him on his toes.::

::It is good you were there.:: Afran's words felt solid in Jae's head. Meaningful. ::She could have fallen in those first flaps of her wings, and littles aren't as unbreakable as they believe themselves to be.::

The sincerity in his words made her eyes water. Simple thanks. Gratitude for the human who could fly.

::She tires.:: Fendellen tipped her head Squirt's way and did something that eased Jae's flight even more. ::I'll hold the center while you turn around me. Afran will make sure the big, bad winter wind doesn't toss anyone from the sky.::

They turned, the two dragons doing most of the work. Jae did little more than float on the lake of air they pushed beneath her wings. She shifted her position a little so the small purple flier caught more updraft as well.

::You sense the air with much skill.:: Afran sounded impressed. ::There are dragons that would do well to learn from you.::

Jae blinked, not sure how to respond.

::Feel proud, youngling.:: Fendellen's words came with softness and a hint of pride. ::He doesn't hand out compliments often, and never when they're not deserved. You will give me a challenge in the skies, I think.::

Jae's cheeks warmed again. She would never challenge a dragon on anything.

::You will need to learn how.:: Afran this time, sounding calm as he flew the outer edge of their gentle turn back toward the village. ::I imagine Irin will recruit you for nursery duties, given that this one has taken to her wings so early.::

She swallowed. ::I would be honored to work with the littles.::

Fendellen snorted. ::I'll remind you of that when one of them has escaped for the hundredth time in a day.::

Jae giggled and looked into Squirt's reckless, delighted eyes. ::You can't be much more work than a baby goat.:: They could climb anything and ate everything.

And looking after them wasn't nearly this much fun.

Squirt wobbled in the sky, and three sets of wings moved to steady the air around her.

::We're nearly back at the village.:: Fendellen rose slightly in the sky. ::Would you like me to scoop her up for the landing?::

Something warm and proud rose in Jae's heart. ::No. I can do it.:: She reached out, waiting for Squirt to notice before she gathered the exhausted small flier into her chest.

Delighting in her useful wings and hands.

CHAPTER 12

Fendellen nosed in through the heavy flaps that kept the nursery closed off from the winter cold. She exhaled into the dim and nodded at the open eye of the yellow dragon keeping watch over his charges. She glanced at the nest where three bodies slept, tangled together in one colorful pile. ::How is Squirt?::

::Tired.::

That was a word that covered many possibilities, but the old dragon didn't sound worried. ::She flew quite the distance today. Even with others holding her air steady, it was quite the feat for one newly hatched.::

::So everyone keeps telling her.:: Kis snorted wryly. ::Her head will be bigger than her body soon, and she won't be able to get off the ground.::

No words could match the joy of a flight in the sky, but she would not remind the old warrior of that. Once, he would have been the skilled flier on the wings of the newest little testing their wings. Instead, he stayed on the ground as others kept his charges safe.

::Your kin did well. Afran tells me she has a sense for the air that he hasn't seen since you took to your wings.::

That was even higher praise than he had given to Jae— and it wasn't wrong. ::She has a feel. One that will only grow as she gains in confidence.::

Kis adjusted his head so he gazed on her with two eyes. ::That's why you're here.::

It was, and it was a little disturbing how easily he still read her thoughts. Queens required privacy.

::You're not queen yet.::

It was good to have someone to remind her of that. Fendellen made her way over to the curve in the wall that had always seemed made just for her and nestled into a ball. Dragon or not, she appreciated the warmth, and a chance to let her thoughts bubble up in peace.

Kis waited silently, just as he'd done when she was a little trying to squirm her way around something difficult. She looked over at his current batch of babies, sound asleep and not yet appreciating just how carefully they were watched and nurtured, and when it was time, pushed out of the nest. Or tucked back into one if they took a headlong flight early, depending on their personality.

Jae wasn't the headlong type. Not unless a Dragon Star was bossing her around, anyhow. ::How do you know when it's time?::

Kis followed her gaze to the hatchlings. He didn't ask her what she meant. ::You will know. Your head will know, and your wisdom.:: He paused. ::Your heart might need some help to get there.::

Her heart squeezed. He had sent forth so many from the nursery, but he would shake off her sympathy, so she didn't offer it. ::Jae is grown in some ways, but not in others.::

::Perhaps.:: He was quiet a while, his eyes bright in the comforting dim. ::You did well, these past two days. She is finding her place in the village, as you intended.::

Keeping anything a secret from the dragon who knew her best was impossible. ::Irin had some thoughts. I just dropped a few words in a few ears.:: Ears that would help Jae understand just how different this village was from the one she grew up in. ::Squirt wasn't part of the plan.::

One of the nestlings stirred and Kis rumbled softly, lulling them back to sleep. ::She needed to feel acceptance from the humans and elves first. And from those who would be her friends.::

She was glad he thought so. Future queens learned not to second-guess their decisions, but it had been tempting to coddle Jae in the safe embrace of the dragons, where her wings were nothing but attraction.

::You let her stand on her own. Meet the village on her own terms. That was well done.::

The warm feeling in her ribs expanded. Kis handed out compliments even more rarely than Afran. ::She wouldn't have trusted the acceptance of the dragons while she still expected the village to be full of those who would fear her.::

::You made the right choice rather than the easy one. It won't be the last time that is required of you.::

It wasn't, and she was here contemplating the next time. ::She's not ready to know I will be queen. Or that we're marked.:: Jae had been so very flustered by all the gratitude when she'd landed with Squirt in her arms.

Kis exhaled slowly. Listening.

Fendellen said the hardest part. ::Jae has spent her whole life wishing to be ordinary.::

::We don't always get what we wish for.:: The words came without emotion, but Fendellen felt them anyhow. ::She does not have the luxury of being ordinary. She is needed.::

Fendellen blew quiet ripples into the nursery air. ::I know.::

::She learns quickly. She did not cower today, or hide her wings.::

Fendellen blinked.

::The kitchen roof is not so far from here. Young Kellan got wind of your schemes and bade me to watch.::

Big, watching yellow heads were hard to hide, but she didn't bother to ask how he'd done it. Or if that had somehow aided Squirt in her escape. None of them had expected the small purple hatchling to fly until spring at the very earliest.

::Irin was watching her.:: Kis sounded amused. ::She shot between his legs when he came in with the breakfast bowls.::

A moment not at all funny when it happened, but one that would gain in humor with each retelling. ::It's been a long time since a hatchling got the jump on him.::

Fondness. ::You might have been the last.::

She'd never gotten very far. What Irin couldn't see coming, his dragon always did. Which is why she was about to make a request that would pain him. ::I'm going to hold a flying class.::

::Good.::

She knew his opinions on flight skills. They had kept him and his kin alive—and perhaps thrust him into the middle of the battle, but knowing his sense of honor, he would have been there anyhow. ::I'm not going to teach it. Not alone, anyhow.::

::Ah.:: A long pause, and then a crisp nod. ::That is wise. You will introduce her to your dragons as a leader. A teacher. Which is not so very different from being kin to a queen.::

And it would provide a decent cover story for the deference they paid their future queen as a matter of due. ::Perhaps she needs more time with the villagers first.::

Kis said nothing, merely blinking slowly in the dim.

An old warrior who knew better than to second-guess one who would be queen. Always, he made her find the firm footing under her own feet and good air currents under her wings. Fendellen shook her head as she found them. ::No. It is time for her to meet the dragons. To begin to understand who they are.:: The kin of a queen would also have a bond with every dragon. Or so they believed. No queen in living memory had chosen a kin.

A low rumble. The closest Kis ever came to approval. ::It will do her good.::

Fendellen tilted her head. Kis often saw much and said little. ::Why do you think so?::

His breath blew into the nursery, fanning the nestlings with warm heat. ::Because they won't think of her as a human with wings.::

Fendellen let her eyelids fall and rise in a slow blink. ::They won't?::

::No.:: He blew warm air over his sleeping charges again. ::She can fly as well or better than any of them. An hour in the sky, and they'll think of her as a dragon with a few missing scales.::

The rightness of that—and the potential hilarity— caught Fendellen's breath.

::You seek to protect her,:: Kis said quietly. ::But also see her. She is star chosen and queen bonded. There are depths to her, strengths we have only begun to see. Be careful that it is not you who ends up holding her back.::

CHAPTER 13

J ae landed on the rock ledge beside the ice-blue dragon, giving all her attention to getting her feet gracefully on the ground, mostly so she could ignore the dozens of eyes watching the two of them.

She wouldn't hide.

Not today. She lowered her wings, but left them hanging wide on her back. She was wearing the new tunic and leggings Alonia had worked so hard on, sewn from the softest, light-blue wool and embroidered with silver thread that matched her feathers. The tunic had a wide slit up the leg, but draped almost to her ankles, and it was the single most beautiful thing Jae had ever seen, much less worn.

She would not hide.

Not while she wore such beautiful clothing made by the hands of a friend, and decorations in her wings, tiny beads that clipped on and caught the light and insisted that she be proud of her feathers because they were beautiful too.

Just getting dressed this morning had been a tangle of emotions, and she was quite sure that journey wasn't over.

::You do them honor with your finery.::

Jae glanced over at the dragon who was somehow hers, but there was no scorn in Fendellen's voice. No sarcasm. ::My friends have been so kind to me.:: She wished they could see this.

::You think they aren't here, child?::

This was a new voice. Jae gaped as a white dragon came up beside her. Old—older than Gran, even. So old that her skin shone like snow about to melt and reveal what lived underneath.

Old, and full of power.

Jae had a sudden urge to fall to her knees, even though she had no idea who the new arrival was.

::That would not be amiss,:: Fendellen said quietly. ::Elhen is our queen.::

A life spent in the high mountains did not prepare anyone to meet royalty. Jae knew there was something known as a curtsy, but she had no earthly idea how to form her body into one. So she turned to the queen. She would pay her respects in the way of the mountains. She dipped her head, in the way of a small plant in a stiff wind. ::May there always be sun to warm you through, my lady.::

"That's a lovely greeting, and a welcome one on such a cold day."

Jae dared a glance up, but the queen didn't look chilled by the temperatures. Dragons would do well in the high country.

Elhen nodded regally. "This isn't an official appearance. I heard word there was to be a flying lesson today, and that it would be worth watching."

Jae's knees turned to springmelt.

::Steady.:: Fendellen's nose touched her shoulder. ::In her day, she was a very fine flier. She is here to watch, and perhaps to remember her youth a little. Not to judge.::

It was so very hard to hold on to the idea that flying was a considered a good thing, worthy of attention and praise. Her conviction kept trying to slip away, a wisp of fog in a stiff breeze.

::There are plenty of stiff breezes this morning.:: Fendellen spread her wings. ::Come. Let's show them what those feathers of yours can do.::

Jae had no idea what that meant, but she followed the ice-blue dragon up into the sky. They weren't alone. Almost every dragon on the ground rose into the air, leaving Elhen on the cliff watching, two dragons flanking her that Jae hadn't even noticed.

::Her guardians.::

Jae twisted around, looking for the enormous gray-black dragon that went with the familiar voice. She spied Afran and tried to avoid looking too closely at the dozens of others in the sky.

::Dragons.:: Fendellen's voice rang with command. ::Form on me. I promised the old man a flyover, and we would do well to get to it before he gets cranky and goes back inside to eat his morning stew.::

Kis. Jae had heard the stories. He would watch them—and he would yearn.

::Yes.:: Fendellen turned in the air, hovering. ::Beside

me, sweet one. You don't belong way back there. It's your tricks the rest will be copying.::

Jae's eyes widened. ::I don't have tricks.::

::You do. And I have a bet going with Elhen that you can make at least one dragon fall out of the sky today, so I want your very best ones.::

Jae wasn't sure whether to be more overwhelmed by the idea of falling dragons or being kin to someone who made bets with royalty. By the time she gave up trying to decide, she was somehow flying at Fendellen's wing tip, a long stream of dragons forming up behind them in the sky.

The ice-blue dragon flew in a lazy circle, tipping her wings at the queen watching below.

Jae dipped her head under her wing and peeked at the line, which was far from the ragged mess it had been before. She could see Afran at the back, a small peach-pink dragon at his side. Lotus. With no Sapphire, which was probably good. Jae had heard some of those stories too, and they generally involved Sapphire ruefully rubbing her backside as she told them.

::A trick, youngling. Something that will look impressive from the ground.::

Nothing came to Jae's dazed mind—until she thought of the eagles. Watching them dive had often made her heart stop.

::Perhaps something a little less likely to put a dragon through a rondo roof.:: Fendellen sounded highly amused.

Jae gulped, her cheeks reddening. Then an entirely different thought came to her. Not eagles this time. Ants, and the intricate patterns they sometimes made when they swarmed. She looked over at Fendellen. ::If I fly a pattern, can you copy me on that side?::

::If I can't, I'll lose my title as the finest flier in the sky.:: The ice-blue dragon didn't sound worried. ::And remember, we're all covered in scales. You're not. Don't let one of these miscreants cause you harm.::

There was a shudder all the way down the long line in the sky. One that made Jae quite certain, for reasons she didn't really understand, that no harm would come to her this day.

Not that she had been worried. She was in the sky with dragons, the sun glinting off the stitching of her tunic and the jewels in her feathers, and none of this felt real at all. Except that it did. It felt like something deep inside her had finally been born, and she was pretty sure her eyes looked very much like Squirt's on her maiden flight.

Full of pure joy.

She flipped over onto her back and zoomed in an undulating circle, picking up speed so the fliers at the back wouldn't have to move too slowly. Fendellen matched her perfectly, mirroring her flight across an invisible line in the sky. Jae made the circle big enough to loop in behind Afran and Lotus, the enormous dragon just as agile as the much smaller one beside him—and far more self-contained.

Jae dipped underneath the line, holding in tight formation just below the other dragons for a moment, and then she split and angled wide and straight up, a climb as steep as she could make it.

She heard the bugling behind her. A dragon horde, ready to charge.

::Ignore them.:: Fendellen arced up gracefully in the

sky, mirroring her flight. ::They're just making sure Kis is awake.::

Kis and anyone else within a full day's journey. Dragons were not quiet, and some of the villagers might still be trying to sleep. Perhaps a human with wings should keep the fliers a little more occupied and a lot less noisy. Jae smiled into the stiff winter wind and angled her wing tips, doing a slow spin as she climbed.

There were several grunts and screeches from the dragons on her heels, and more than one in Fendellen's train fell out of line. Jae stiffened and stopped her spin. She hadn't meant to cause trouble.

::That's exactly what I meant for you to do.:: Fendellen sounded stern, like the village teacher when someone might be thinking about misbehaving. ::It's not trouble. It will give them something to strive for. And some are managing just fine.::

Jae looked over to discover that the ice-blue dragon had not stopped her spin as she climbed—and some of the dragons behind her were indeed managing. The ones that weren't circled and came up near the end, closer to Afran.

There was another bugle from beneath her. An impatient one this time.

Jae laughed. Apparently dragons were just small children with wings and scales.

::And fire breath,:: Fendellen added, clearly amused.

Jae winced and switched to a spiraling climb instead, one that let her build up some speed and hopefully avoided scorched wings. She kept it looping and big, delighting in the buffeting of the winds and watching the dragons below. They were magnificent, their scales shining in the sun as they formed a magical tunnel in the sky.

She grinned, positioned herself carefully over the middle of the tunnel, and tucked her wings in, leaving only the tips for flying. Then she dropped down inside the spiral—not as fast as a dive, but fast enough to send her heart racing. She whooped as she fell, just like the children of the mountains did when they raced down the slides of ice.

Bugling answered her from every direction, including right above her head.

::Now would be a bad time to stop.:: Fendellen sounded excited and a little short of breath. ::There would be a pileup.::

Jae giggled. That happened on the ice slides too. She tucked into a ball and flipped over, her head pointing straight at the ground. Then she zoomed out the bottom of the tunnel and into the bright sky.

Just in time to get out of the way of the chaos.

Dragons ran into each other like rocks tumbling down a steep hill, some falling headfirst, some tail first, and some spinning off to try to find their bearings in less-occupied skies.

Jae squeaked and pulled in a wing as a green dragon hurtled past, clearly not at all sure which way was up.

Then there was an ice-blue dragon at her side, and probably more usefully, a huge dark-gray bulk right over her head. Protecting her, just like they had done with Squirt.

Fendellen trumpeted, a sound that had no words but was clearly an order.

The chaos instantly dimmed as dragons formed themselves into a huge circle in the sky. Afran joined the ring, leaving just the two of them in the center.

Fendellen snorted, pivoting slowly. ::If you were looking to impress my kin with your flying prowess, that was rather poorly done.::

Even while flying, tails somehow drooped.

Fendellen looked pointedly at Jae. ::She will now demonstrate that trick again.::

Jae stared. She wasn't quite sure which one had caused all the chaos.

::The one where you flipped head over tail, youngling.:: Afran sounded amused. ::It is perhaps trickier when you have a tail.::

::Says the dragon who managed it better than any of the others.:: Fendellen snorted gently at Jae. ::Go ahead. They can likely manage to watch without flying into each other.::

Jae shook her head. As lessons went, this one was clearly a disaster.

::It's nothing of the sort.:: The ice-blue dragon flicked a wing. ::Go on. We're going to master this, and then Kis might be truly impressed by what he sees in the sky.::

There were shadows under Fendellen's words. She worried about the old dragon.

Jae squared her shoulders. She would do what she could to ease Kis's pain. She angled her wings and flapped enough to lift herself a short way. Then, as slowly as she could, she tucked and rotated into the beginning of a dive she never let get underway.

Fendellen studied every feather intently. ::Again. A little faster this time.::

Jae climbed a little higher and repeated it, this time shooting out right under an ice-blue tail. ::It's easier if you go faster.::

::It's easier if you go faster and do the right things,:: Fendellen said dryly. She flicked a wing again. ::Go over by Afran. I don't want to knock you out of the sky with a wild tail.::

Jae scooted out of the way as the ice-blue dragon's intentions became clear. And stared as Fendellen's first roll was a tumble of wings and tail and an exit that shot straight toward a group of dragons who hastily scooted out of the way.

Then Fendellen gathered herself, turned around, and faced Jae expectantly.

::She awaits your suggestions.:: Afran hovered behind her as easily as a hummingbird. ::For how she can improve.::

Jae wasn't sure she had any that would work for a dragon. ::It's easier if you're falling. Then you can feel the pull of the ground.::

::Ah.:: Fendellen flapped hard straight up into the sky. Then she tucked in her wings just as Jae had done at the top of the tunnel.

Jae held her breath as ice-blue limbs and scales tucked and rolled, but this time, Fendellen flipped neatly and came out in a dive pointed straight at the ground. One she zoomed out of with a blast of fire that echoed the glee Jae could feel in her head.

::That is the bond between you.::

Jae heard the huge dragon's words, and somehow, here up in the sky, knew them to be true in a way that didn't make sense on the ground.

::Much easier at speed.:: Fendellen pulled up sharply in front of them, eyes gleaming. Then she spun around to face the rest of the dragons.

Jae winced as she imagined dozens of dragons all hurtling toward the ground at the same time. She skimmed forward to Fendellen's shoulder. ::Perhaps we can do a circle. Or hills and valleys.:: She moved her hand to show what she meant.

::The youngling is wise.:: Afran turned his head toward the sun. ::And it will move us toward the village.::

Fendellen flew forward, and like a well-organized herd of goats, the dragons fell in line behind her. The ice-blue dragon nodded to the empty skies in front of her. ::Lead us, sweet one. You tumble, and we will follow.::

Jae was sure her rightful place was anywhere but at the front of the line, but perhaps she would be safest there. She sailed into the lead, wings wide and gleaming in the sun and pride ballooning in her heart.

And then she pointed her nose at the horizon and flew. Up imaginary hills and down, tumble-rolling on the downhills and zooming back up them, whooping as loudly as she wanted because one human couldn't possibly be heard over the cacophony of dragons behind her.

On the third hill, she remembered she was not a child ice-sliding in the sky, but a teacher, and she changed the roll to a twist. Lotus barrel rolled through the village easily enough. Perhaps that one would be easier for dragons.

The next hill, she stretched out her wings and did a

graceful swan dive toward the snow, one that ended in a snap of wings and a very sharp change of direction.

::Those will do nicely.:: Afran's calm approval sounded in her head. ::By the time we reach the village, each dragon will have mastered at least one of those. The one right behind you needs another hill or two to have all three.::

Jae beamed into the weak winter sun. Her dragon was a magnificent flier.

A long, quiet pause. And then, through the bond between them, sheer happiness. ::That's the first time you have called me your dragon.::

Jae nodded slowly, even though Fendellen couldn't see. And tried to feel worthy.

::This isn't something you earn.:: Afran again, gentle and steady and wise. ::But I think maybe you have nonetheless. She follows very few.::

Jae's wings spluttered. ::She put me up front to keep me safe.::

::No, youngling. She put you up front so you can shine as you're meant to.::

Cold fingers of denial tightened around Jae's heart—and then the bond inside her pulsed, warm and fierce, and pushed the cold back.

Jae tumbled down another imaginary hill in the sky.

And shone.

CHAPTER 14

*J*ae hugged the precious piece of paper to her chest, and the even more precious sachets of herbs that had come with it. Gran had also sent a jar of the oil she used when Jae's feather shafts got dry and brittle in the winter.

Gifts that said as much as the words that came with them.

The letter was written in Mellie's hand. Gran had grown up long before schooling and teachers had come to the high mountains, and she always said that she wrote what she needed to remember right inside her own head. So the careful script was Mellie's—Gran's only apprentice now—but the sentiments were all those of the old woman who had taken Jae in and raised her.

To my Jae. The man with the boots too thin for a mountain winter tells me you have arrived safely in a village of dragons and those who care for them. I cannot say whether such a thing is real or not, but he assures me he is not a demon, and he gave me the letter and the dried wintergreen you sent. I don't know where you found such treasure in mid-winter, but my hands thank you. I will make a fever oil for the babies with it.

The man also tried to give me coins, but what use do I have for such things here? I have sent them back with him, in case they might aid in your care and keeping, even though I know that will not be necessary. You are a hard worker, and he assured me they are in need of healing skills.

I have sent your warm winter cloak, and a few of the medicines every healer needs. The man assures me you will come visit in spring to pick up more.

Stay safe, daughter of my hands. I would see you again.

Jae knew what the last words said, but she could no longer see them. Tears pricked her eyes, as they had every time she read them. The young dragon kin who had delivered the message had been shivering with cold, and she had not begged him for more news from her village. That could wait until he ate some stew and slept. His journey must have been long and cold, even by dragon flight.

She stroked a finger over the sachets. Chamomile and swampcress and the dark purple berries that made the best syrup for winter coughs. Love, in the way Gran knew best how to say it.

Jae sniffled. She would collect more wintergreen. It grew here, even in the cold. Alonia had shown her where to find a patch, and Inga had let her use a corner of the kitchen to dry it. She had sent a feather, too, one with pretty beads threaded in. Gran would know what it meant.

Here, she did not need to hide.

She cuddled deeper into the straw in the corner of the nursery and wrapped herself a little tighter in the cloak that smelled of home. The babies hadn't stirred when she'd come in to watch over them, and neither had the great yellow dragon, but she had no doubts that Kis was aware of her presence.

She'd needed somewhere safe and warm to think, and her rondo was too big and empty. It hadn't felt quite so big when she'd napped against Fendellen's chest before dinner, but her dragon had gone off to the caves to speak to the queen and left an echoing chamber behind her. To someone used to a small hut in the mountains full of medicines and baskets and often cranky patients, it had been the wrong place to think. And Jae needed, so very much, to do some thinking.

These last days had been a storm. A wonderful one, full of acceptance and lifting winds and new friends. But still a storm, and her body ached with the efforts of tumbling down sky hills and walking through a village with her wings out for all to see.

Gran always said that once a storm was done, the calm was a good time to gather the medicines you would need for the next one. Jae didn't need medicines, but she needed to take the experiences and feelings in her belly and let them steep to see what came out in the brew.

Part of what she needed was the settling of a good dose of chamomile. There had been kindness and joy and exhilaration and easy acceptance in these days, and they had tossed her about like the winds in a high mountain pass. Or like the sights and sounds at a festival market, so big and brash and overwhelming.

She had flown in the sky with bugling dragons. Even

Gran would deem that worthy of a stiff cup of chamomile tea.

She smiled as one of the baby dragons snuffled in sleep and cuddled in closer to her companions. Three born knowing they were accepted and loved. They would never feel the bone-deep doubt that came from being left on a mountainside to die. None of Gran's teas had ever been able to make that go away, or treat the creeping poison that had snuck in a little further every time Jae bound her wings and hid them under her cloak.

She let the tears fall. Let herself truly feel the weight of those bindings now that she could finally let them go.

She hadn't known how heavy they were.

Her feathers wrapped around her, light and soft and bearing witness to the joy of flying in the light even while she huddled in the warm dark. When she had led the line of dragons over the village, Fendellen on her heels, she had felt like a queen. There had been so many people standing between the rondos, all waving and smiling and pointing at the fliers in the sky.

Her new friends had waved the most wildly of all.

Then Fendellen had whispered into her head, and she had led a tumbling, twisting, swan-diving line of dragons right over the big rondo where Kis lived. The huge yellow dragon had stood solemnly and watched them, and if he felt pain and longing, it hadn't shown.

All she had felt was his pride.

For her, and for the ice-blue dragon on her heels.

Which was part of what she needed to add to her stew of thoughts and feelings, because more was going on here than she understood. The careful looks that had nothing to do with her wings. The way the dragons deferred to Fendellen when it was very clear they were a pack of unruly children the rest of the time. The part of her that suspected the last two days were not accidental, but instead a lesson, carefully planned and even more carefully delivered.

A welcome for her, most surely. But it felt like something else, too. A readying.

Jae exhaled quietly into the dim as the ingredients of her brew steeped themselves into a well-mixed tea. To be kin to a dragon could not possibly be a small thing. It must come with responsibilities, just like those of a healer's apprentice, but she didn't know her job in this new world. Or what medicines she might need to have on hand to tend to her new life's bumps and bruises.

She nodded, her path decided. This was a fine first tea, but she needed more ingredients to make the next. More understanding. More information.

This village didn't have a healer, and the resident storyteller was a dragon, so her usual ways to gather what she needed wouldn't work here. Alonia knew something, and maybe Kellan too, but tricking a friend into speaking out of turn wasn't nice, and those two had been nothing but kind.

She would have to do as Gran taught her on their first gathering trips in the high mountains. Watch. Take small bites. Listen to the secrets in the wind.

She folded the precious letter in her lap carefully. It had taken great effort to deliver it to her hands, and she would treasure it and not let too many tears fall to blur the words. Instead, she would begin collecting medicines for spring. Fendellen had nuzzled her cheek right before she headed for the caves, and promised they would fly north as soon as the snows melted.

Jae swallowed. She would not be able to take her dragon to her village, and that was a sadness that added bitterness to her tea. But her mountains would welcome the ice-blue dragon, and her winds would play with the two of them in the skies, and she would find a way to let Fendellen and Gran look into each other's eyes.

She would honor her old life when the spring melts came. Until then, she would learn what she could of the new one. Including the parts that were tucked out of easy view. Healers knew that was often where the most precious medicines grew.

And sometimes where the harshest dangers lurked.

But she was a child of the mountains, and a hard worker to boot, and she would not shirk away from what had chosen her. Not when it came with so much light. She smiled and snuggled down a little deeper into her cloak—and caught sight of a large golden eye watching her in the dark.

Awake and serene and maybe even approving.

INTERLUDE

Lovissa shook her head as yet another dragon zoomed through the valley, tumbling and turning and narrowly avoiding rocks and trees, to say nothing of the assembled audience. The previous two fliers had not been so lucky. They were currently nursing bumps and bruises by the healing fire Baret had hastily set up out of the way of the chaos.

As well she might have. Many of the tumbling dragons were her charges.

Led by one tiny, mighty purple-gray dragon who would one day be queen.

Baraken landed on the cliff's edge beside her. ::Quira says she learned this in dream.::

And he was a wise enough warrior to understand the implications of that. ::There is a fourth who has been marked by the Dragon Star. Not an elf this time. A human. With wings.::

Her steadiest warrior startled beside her.

::Her dragon has not yet told her of the star's choosing.::

A long pause. ::Is that wise?::

Lovissa sighed. It was a good question, and one with no easy answer. ::The flying human is kin to Fendellen.:: Baraken had great respect for the ice-blue dragon who would come.

His great head nodded slowly. ::She is young, but she does not make decisions rashly.::

He might change his mind about that shortly. ::It is her flying kin who is teaching this tumbling to the dragons Quira sees in her dreams.::

His snort of surprise billowed out into the chill air. ::She is a flier of some skill, then.::

If dream told true. ::She flies as the eagles do, and the hawks. And with the joy of a hatchling who has just discovered her wings.:: It was both difficult to watch and utterly captivating.

Baraken winced as yet another dragon tried the head-to-tail roll and landed himself in a much-mangled tree. ::So Quira flies as the kin of Fendellen flies.::

It was an apt comparison. And one with weight she had not yet fully thought through. ::Of the dragons who will come, there are only two who can match our Quira.:: A point of pride for Lovissa—and one that suddenly tickled her sense of humor. ::One is Fendellen. The other is Afran.:: The enormous gray dragon of Baraken's line.

The warrior beside her stiffened. He knew a challenge when he heard one.

Lovissa watched, regal and amused, as Quira zoomed through the valley again, flipping and twisting and putting all the much larger dragons to shame. The littles were learning these tricks far faster than those fully grown—perhaps because they did not yet understand just how difficult such maneuvers should be.

Or because the grown dragons weren't wise enough to study the lithely tumbling littles.

The dragon beside her did not make that mistake. His eyes tracked Quira as she rolled and zoomed in the sky.

Good queens rewarded diligence. ::The human winged one says the roll is easiest while falling. It helps to feel the pull of the earth in the turning.::

Amusement flashed in Baraken's eyes. ::Does the human winged one have any idea how much damage an overly fast dragon landing can cause?::

::No. She is a creature of much innocence.::

Baraken shot her a sharp look. ::Bonded to one who will be queen?::

They had come so very far that he could tolerate the idea of a kin-bonded dragon at all. For her, that acceptance came slowly, one dream fragment at a time. For him, perhaps it came one broken dragonkiller arrow at a time. ::The star has chosen. It is not for me to question.:: That would not be enough for her finest warrior, but it was the only answer the dreams had given.

She did, however, have something to give him that he would cherish. ::The dragons to come have three new hatchlings. They have been gifted with a special one.::

His eyes softened. The last special one of this Veld, so ancient she could no longer make fire, had stood over him as he hatched. ::This new one—she has guardians?::

That was the part she offered to him as treasure. ::Yes. Two. A dark purple hatchling who has already found her wings. And a warrior.:: She turned and looked straight into Baraken's eyes. ::His scales match your own.::

His breath caught.

She nodded, formal and regal, acknowledging the service of his line across time. ::One who comes from you. He does you honor.::

Her warrior straightened, strengthened by her words, as she had intended. A queen's gifts were not given lightly, and they were never simple.

She had just given the dragon she faced yet another reason to sustain the peace—and to fight fiercely and well if it failed.

She nodded her head toward the valley. ::Go. Show the younglings how it's done.::

He lifted his wings and met her gaze a moment longer before he took to the sky in pursuit of a small purple-gray lightning bolt.

Lovissa stirred.

This was dream, but strange dreaming. It called to the line of queens in her blood, as the ashes did. But it did not call her to fire. This place was cold. Eternally so, with nothing but points of light breaking up the blanket of dark.

In this dream, she walked the skies.

She was not alone. Another shape, familiar and eerie, walked a path through the stars that would intersect with hers.

She inclined her head, acknowledging Elhen. The old dragon nodded back, her moves slow and regal. If she was awed by this walk through the stars, she did not show it.

::I have come here before.:: The words were solemn. Steady. ::I have not seen one of your time here.::

Somehow, Lovissa knew the answer to that. ::We go to the ashes to speak to the queens who have come before us. You have no ashes to visit.::

::I do not.:: Deep sadness—and acceptance. ::You are fortunate to have such wisdom within your reach.::

One who honored her line, even if she could not talk to their ashes. ::There is much happening in your time. The new winged one grows in strength.::

A long silence as they walked side by side bathed in starlight. ::The one who will be queen after me has greatness in her, and also great vulnerability. Jae is a gift, if Fendellen can learn to accept all of what she brings. A time of upheaval comes. I would wish, with all that is in me, that Fendellen would not walk that path alone.::

Only a very few could understand the vast loneliness of a queen's calling. ::You believe the winged one is strong enough to stand with her?::

::The star believes.::

Perhaps. It was not for queens to understand the motives of stars. ::Or perhaps she is needed for other reasons.::

Sadness. ::Perhaps.::

Lovissa had no wisdom to offer to such sadness—but she did have a gift. ::You have a small purple one who does not yet have a name.::

Elhen's gaze quickened with interest. ::Yes. The one who is called Squirt.::

A nickname that gained in accuracy by the day, but it did not capture the fullness of a young dragon who would be a special one's guardian. ::We lost a fine warrior in battle this summer past. She was brought down by dragonkiller arrows.:: A wish, sharp as a sword, stabbed Lovissa's chest, that no more would have to die.

::She fought so that others might live.::

Lovissa dipped her head. ::You have one who paid with his wings to do the same.::

This time, the aching sadness had layers. A queen who mourned for a warrior and a friend.

Lovissa was glad. Perhaps the old white queen did not walk entirely alone. ::The dragon who was lost was one of much joy and spirit. Her name was Eleret. I would be well pleased to think her reborn in a time of peace.::

::Eleret.:: Elhen murmured the name to the stars, and the stars murmured it back. ::It will take her a while to grow into it yet, but it fits her.::

::Then it shall be so.:: Two queens walking the stars could surely decide that much.

And perhaps it would ease the other decision weighing on Elhen's wings.

PART III
TWO HEARTS TRUE

CHAPTER 15

*J*ae juggled her cloak, two bowls of stew, a knife with a loose handle, and the pot of salve she'd just finished making, and tried to free up a hand to open the door to the nursery. There were days when an extra pair of hands would be far more useful than wings.

She used her feathers to shelter the stew and the salve, trying to hold some heat in both. It was a clear, crisp day, but the wind said something was building up in the weather again. She reached out for Fendellen's mind, something that was getting easier with practice. ::Tell those practicing their flying to be careful. The winds will make the rolling fun, but also more dangerous.::

::You don't say,:: came the dry reply.

Jae made a face, even though her dragon couldn't see it. ::I'm sorry. I didn't think to warn you.::

::I've been flying as long as you have and Afran far longer. We shouldn't need warnings.::

That sounded dire. ::Do you need a healer?::

::Mostly for our pride. We're fine, sweet one, and we'll make sure the others don't collect more than a few bumps and bruises. Are you done with your potion?::

::I am. Now I just have to figure out how to get the door open with my hands full of all the things people needed delivered to the nursery.::

Amusement, and warmth. ::None of them wanted to venture out into the cold.::

Evidently not. ::They'd never last in the high mountains.::

::You're made of sterner stuff, my sweet kin. Back away from the door a bit. Irin is coming to let you in.::

Jae blinked, but she took a step back just as the door cracked and the weapons master stuck his head out. He took one look at the pile in her arms and understood the problem. He reached first for the knife, carefully extracting it by its handle, and then took one of the bowls of stew. "Come in. Kis will be glad to see his breakfast. The hatch-lings ate most of what I had set aside for this morning."

Jae halted as the door swung shut behind her and three dragon babies with very sharp claws tried to climb her legs.

Kis rumbled, low and stern, and they all promptly dropped to the floor and sat, chastened.

Irin gave all three a look. "That stew she's holding would be *my* breakfast, you never-ending buckets of hunger."

Jae hid a smile as Eleret's dark purple eyebrow ridges drooped sadly. Her new name had come in the night, a message from far-off lands, and it suited her. "I could go to the kitchen for more. Kellan said they were making two pots full."

"They're still babies enough that their bellies need milk curds." Irin dropped a small spoonful of stew in a bowl on top of a pile of the soft white cheese. Then he set it down in front of her toes.

Jae watched with interest as Eleret and Taenin nudged their yellow friend toward the bowl first. Mountain families often shared from one dish too, but it was rare for the littles to delay their own feeding to care for another. Gran would approve. Such lessons ran far deeper than feeding. She glanced at Irin. "How do they know to care for Rilli so well?" It certainly wasn't that way in human villages, even when revered healers led the way. It took attentiveness and sometimes threats to make sure the sick and the weak got what they needed to survive to the next spring melts.

"Elhen says their blood knows." Irin took a seat and stuck the spoon back in his bowl, this time to feed himself. "Whatever it is, I'm glad of it."

Jae had no doubt he would have used his blade to defend the small yellow dragon, but it didn't seem necessary. It made her heart glad. She set the pot of salve she carried down next to the knife he had taken from her hands. "Karis said you would know what to do for the knife. The salve is for Kis. If you rub it on the sorest parts of his wings, it should ease the pain some."

Irin's eyebrows flew up into his hairline. "You seem quite sure of that."

Jae shrugged. "It works on everyone from humans to goats, and one time Gran even used it on a bear."

Irin's cheek twitched. "That must be quite a story."

It wasn't a long one. "She found a young one in a cave, nursing a leg that had been caught in a trap. The cave was near the growing slopes of a flower we needed to make the coughing medicine, so it was only right to help heal the bear so it could leave and let us gather the flowers in peace."

A long pause. "Your gran comes from sturdy stock."

That was a compliment Gran would enjoy. "She has a way with animals. She returned three times with more salve for the bear. The fourth time we went, it was gone."

Irin regarded the salve pot, this time with strong interest. "Kis can be about as grumpy as a bear, so perhaps this will help ease his winter aches. Thank you, missy. It's a very thoughtful thing you did to make it."

Another low rumble. ::I would add my thanks, youngling.::

Jae felt her cheeks warm. "It's a simple salve. One of the first an apprentice learns to make."

"It's the simplest ones that are often the most useful." Irin picked up the pot and gave it a sniff. "Comfrey, and chamomile, but I don't recognize the rest."

She blinked. She hadn't known he was a healer too. "I don't know what you call the other. It's got five leaves that curl tightly at night and a dark purple blossom, but it's just the leaves that go in the salve."

Irin shook his head. "I'm just the soldier who knows how to grind up the things I'm told to use. Alonia and Trift would know if it grows around here, though." His eyes narrowed. "Is this what you did with the dried packets that came with your letter?"

She nodded, able to hear the edge in his tone, but not

understanding it. "Some of them." Most of them. Dragons were big.

He huffed out a breath. "Your generosity does you credit, missy."

She shrugged. "He needs it most."

"Indeed." He set the pot back down on the table. "I'm grateful."

Two quietly spoken words, but they warmed her all the way to her belly. The high mountains never took their healers for granted, but she rarely felt quite this appreciated.

Jae jumped at a crash behind her.

Irin stood up, ire in his eyes. "Not in the nursery, missy. Wings are for using outside and under strict supervision."

He didn't mean her. He meant the small purple dragon rubbing her head on her wing. The one she had clearly just run into the back of the door. Jae winced. She'd hit a tree once, back when she was learning to fly. She'd had a big bump for a week. "I can take her outside and supervise."

"Once it's warmer." Irin's frown didn't ease, but she had the distinct sense he didn't mean much by it. "And once those infernal dragons aren't flipping themselves around in the sky."

The last words were said quietly, for her ears alone.

She shot a quick glance at Kis. Pains came in some forms salves couldn't heal. Perhaps it hurt him too much, watching the antics of the other dragons.

"Not him." Irin sat back down on his stool. "He might not admit it, but he enjoys seeing the fliers put through their paces. And it amuses him that it's a puny human doing it."

There was no point arguing—she was puny. "Fendellen and Afran are very good."

"He was better." A simple statement, said with no boasting at all. "You remind him of what he once was, and I thank you for that." He shot a wry look at Eleret, still rubbing her head. "However, those tricks also tempt little ones who can't even fly in straight lines yet. Best she stays inside until the skies are more sedate."

Jae wasn't sure that would work. Littles didn't tend to forget the things you wanted them to. "I need to go help Kellan with the next pot of stew." Inga had discovered that her wings could fan the fire without blowing ashes all over the kitchen, and stews liked a good, hot fire.

Irin inclined his head. "Thank you for the breakfast."

She smiled. It was nice to feel useful. "I've got some set aside for Fendellen too. Although someone always seems to remember to feed her."

"Indeed they do." Irin's voice was casual as he picked up the knife with the loose handle.

A man who wasn't going to drop any easy clues.

Jae stood. She wouldn't pry further. She'd already picked up a nugget or two in the kitchen, and perhaps more would come her way as she chopped vegetables for Kellan's magic pot.

She waved to the babies and stepped out the door, making sure to keep wind out and dragons in. Then she crossed the short, blustery way to the kitchen. She'd almost made it back into warm and cozy when two voices hailed her. Karis and Ana, trying to batten down one of the thick waterproof cloths that covered the large entryways into many of the rondos. This one had caught in the wind, and they were struggling to get it back into place.

She wrapped her wings tightly around her as she made her way to where they stood, their arms folded as they glared at the cloth.

Jae could see the problem. She could feel it. The wind bent around the kitchen rondo and whistled by at just the angle to pin the cloth to the rondo wall. Very effective if it was already closed, but letting a nasty wind inside now that it had been forced open.

"We've tried rolling it," said the wagon master crossly. "But two of us aren't strong enough."

Ten of them wouldn't be strong enough. Not in this wind. "You need to redirect the air. Just for a minute so it will let go of the cloth."

Karis raised an eyebrow. "Like a windblock?"

She'd been thinking of wings, but hers weren't big enough. She knew someone's who were, though. ::Fendellen? Can you come help us close a door?::

She felt the assent from her dragon rather than heard it.

Karis flashed a grin. "That will work, although my windblock is bigger."

Ana stared. "You called *Fendellen* to come block the wind so we could close a door?"

Jae wasn't sure why the wagon master sounded so surprised. "It should work."

"Oh, it will work." Ana started to laugh, and then looked at Karis and sobered abruptly. "It will work just fine. Thank you, youngling."

Jae stashed that into her box of odd happenings. More

ingredients for her next pot of tea. She turned, looking for the incoming ice-blue dragon.

And blinked at Fendellen's terrifying speed.

::The little one. Jae, can you catch her?::

Karis hissed and pointed, but Jae had already spied Eleret's small purple form streaking through the skies well above the rondo roofs.

Far higher than she was permitted to fly.

She shed her cloak and flapped, heedless of the blast of air she left behind her as she took off into the stiff, buffeting wind. The air over the village was a nasty mix of incoming storm and rising heat from the rondos—and she saw the moment Eleret ran into trouble.

The small purple body pitched and tossed, the hatchling screeching as she lost control of her wild flight and tumbled toward the ground.

Jae dove. Fendellen was closer, but she was too big to dive between the rondos. Irin ran, but his warrior legs weren't going to arrive in time. She was the only one who was maybe close enough.

The wind was like thick snow, impeding her flight, pushing her back.

Jae reached, stretching out her hands with everything in her, and cried out in horror as Eleret crashed to the ground—just beyond her outstretched fingertips.

CHAPTER 16

"Don't move her." Jae held up a hand and used the voice Gran pulled out when she needed people to listen most. "If her bones are out of place, we could hurt her more."

That was the most frightening possible problem, but in this wind, there were other dangers too. Jae looked up, seeking the eyes of her dragon. "I need dragons to block the wind and to warm the air around her, if you can do that carefully."

::I can.:: A golden eye, filled with remorse, looked over Fendellen's shoulder. ::I didn't see her leave.::

"Not your fault, old man. You were napping. This is on me." Irin looked ready to fight six battles at once. He looked straight at Jae. "What do you need, healer?"

She was only an apprentice, but in the high mountains, she was also often all that was available. "Blankets. Hot water. Some small, strong boards and ties."

"Splints." He nodded and started pointing fingers and

issuing terse instructions. She heard footsteps running away.

The wind died off sharply. Dragon windbreak firmly in place, and Irin seemed more than competent to take care of the rest of what she would need. Jae put her attention in her hands. One, she rested ever so gently on Eleret's chest, checking her breathing. With the other, she poked and prodded as gingerly as she could, feeling for bones that had moved from where they belonged.

She checked the neck first, which was the most fragile part of humans caught in snow slides and rock crevices. Her fingers found nothing, but it worried her that Eleret hadn't moved at all.

::I can still feel her strongly.:: Fendellen was a column of ice-blue calm. ::She isn't the first hatchling to fall from the sky. Young dragons have soft bones. We mend easily and well.::

The intensity swirling all around her said differently, but Jae couldn't let that touch her. A scared healer was one who made mistakes. "What are the most common injuries when they fall?"

Silence, but she could hear words that didn't quite reach her head, as if dragons were talking all at once, but on the other side of a wall. Then Fendellen spoke again, still a column of calm. "Bumps on heads that swell for a few days. Wings that are bent out of shape, sometimes quite sharply. Irin knows how to splint a wing."

She glanced up at the weapons master. "Check her wings." Hurts there wouldn't be as dangerous, but she didn't want to move Eleret until they knew as much as possible about her injuries.

The older man's hands were brisk and gentle. He'd obviously done this before. Jae kept feeling gingerly under the small purple body.

Eleret's whimper nearly cracked through her calm.

Irin's hands stilled. "Here. It's hot to my touch. This is the wing that landed first."

Jae let herself see the terrible crash in her mind. "Wing, and then her head."

"How is her neck?" Irin spoke so quietly, Jae was certain no one else could hear him.

"Nothing obviously wrong," she replied, just as quietly. They could still tie the little body to a board before they moved her, but even with Kis blowing flame over their heads, the air was chill. Jae swallowed and made the hard decision with brisk confidence, just as she'd been taught. She looked at Irin and his big hands. "Can you carry her? We can fold her wings around her, but the most important part is to keep her head from moving around too much."

"We have everything ready." A new voice, Karis this time. "In the nursery. It's a little farther to walk, but there's more room."

Irin nodded, his hands already moving into position beside Eleret's body.

Jae could see his intent. They would roll the baby dragon away and then back onto his hands, as if they were a board. She nodded and folded Eleret's wings, taking extra care with the sore spot. The tiny dragon stirred anyhow.

Jae knew the wing was the least of their worries. A little of the salve she had brought to Kis would make that right in no time.

"Her tail." Fendellen's breath was hot on her shoulders.

Kellan squatted beside them. "I can lift it at the same time as you lift her body. I can tuck it into Irin's arms."

The tail still held bones. Flexible ones, but they would connect to the tiny dragon's neck. Jae shook her head. "I think it's better if you walk with us. Keep it as level with her body as you can. No bending." She could see the sharply attentive calm of a very good helper in Kellan's eyes as her friend nodded. They had the team who would move the baby. Now all they needed was a traveling windbreak.

::It's all ready.:: Fendellen's ice-blue wings rose behind Irin's back. ::We have dragons two layers deep blocking the wind from all directions.::

Jae nodded. Three sets of eyes met. As one unit, they rose to their feet, Irin's hands supporting most of Eleret's weight, Kellan and Jae managing wings and tail.

Two hands landed on Jae's hips. "Let me guide you." Karis applied gentle pressure to illustrate her words. "That way, Irin can walk forward, and you don't need to look."

That was a trick Jae hadn't used before, but it was a smart one for a short distance. Slowly, she took a step, Irin and Kellan mirroring her moves. She kept her strides short and rhythmic, and her eyes on her patient. If Eleret stirred now, it would likely do more harm than good.

She breathed out as they entered the warm dim of the nursery. Or rather, the warm brightness. Someone had set out many candles around a small bed of straw on the floor.

Ana stood by the straw. "Would you like a blanket laid down, healer?"

Another one with sharply attentive calm in her eyes. "Yes, please." Jae assumed it would be old, clean, and not very precious. This village had survived without an official healer for a long time. They knew what to do.

A small square of wool whisked out over the straw, Ana smoothing out the wrinkles before she stepped back, well out of their way. The trio holding Eleret moved into position and lowered her carefully, their unison as tight as the mountain rescue teams who practiced such things together every fortnight.

Kellan let out a soft breath as Eleret settled on the blanket-covered straw. Jae carefully rolled the small body one more time to extract Irin's hands, and then she had her patient settled in warmth and safety, which was every healer's first goal.

Her very still patient.

A human child still for this long would be very worrisome indeed. Soft bones might not break, but the ones of the head and neck could damage in ways that couldn't be fixed.

Irin and Kellan remained close, clearly ready to be helpful if they were needed.

Some rustling from the direction of the door, and then Alonia and Inga arrived, bearing bowls and plates. Inga nodded crisply. "Warm broth, good for dragons, even the small ones. Bread and cheese and tea for the healers. Some toasted curds, which this little one especially likes."

All good things for when Eleret woke up.

Jae started feeling her way around the small purple head, her fingers seeking more sore spots. Some kind of reason for so much stillness.

Another stir, and more rustling. This time it wasn't cooks who approached. It was Rilli and Taenin, the two hatchlings walking very slowly, their gazes glued to their small friend.

Jae wasn't sure what to do. Children were rarely allowed near patients, but Gran had made exceptions when they were well behaved and important to the one who was hurt. This seemed to qualify. She reached for Fendellen in her head. ::Can you tell them to be very careful, and only touch her with their noses?::

::Already done. Kis and Afran are each minding one. Dragons often lie with those who are hurt. If it won't get in your way, they would like to do that. Perhaps by her tail.::

That would work, but it wasn't Eleret's tail that was hurt. ::Up by her head, I think. I don't need much room to work, and it will do her good to sense their breathing.::

Warm approval from her dragon.

Jae kept up the movement of her fingers—and then jumped when her patient sneezed. A black nose and a yellow one immediately darted closer.

Eleret didn't move again, but her breathing quickened into a rhythm that looked a lot more like sleeping hatchling than senseless one. Jae swallowed. She had no idea what was good and normal, so she would just need to trust her eyes and hands to guide her. Nothing on Eleret's head seemed to be sore, which was a small miracle.

She glanced over at Irin. "Can you put some of Kis's salve on the sore spot on her wing? A good, thick layer, if she can be trusted not to lick it off." She knew from experience just how hard wings were to bandage.

Sapphire put the pot in his hands before he could do anything more than nod.

So many helpers. So many worried eyes watching one small hatchling.

A small whimper as Irin worked salve over the sprained wing.

::Perhaps where it joins her body, too.:: Kis hadn't taken his eyes off the two dragonets lying quietly at Eleret's head. ::If she landed on her wing, that will be where the soreness comes tomorrow.::

Of course. She should have thought of that. Jae nodded, both in remorse and thanks.

::You're doing very well.:: A long pause. ::Many are not so calm when a young one is hurt. You have set a tone they can all follow. You and your dragon both. It is well done.::

Jae hadn't even thought about how worried the dragons must be, and most of them wouldn't be able to fit inside the rondo. She ran her hands over the small, scaled body again. Eleret seemed warm enough, and she already knew that dragons hated covers of any kind.

::She doesn't feel cold.:: Fendellen seemed quite certain of that.

Jae blinked. It wasn't the first time her dragon had claimed such intimate knowledge of Eleret's state, but it was the first time she was able to pay attention. ::How can you feel her so easily?::

A longer pause. ::It is a bond some dragons have with others. Mine are particularly strong. I can feel the strength of her heart, and her feelings. She hurts some, but I believe that part of her is also still trying to fly.::

Patients often had strange dreams and hallucinations,

but they usually came with fever. Perhaps the room was too warm. Jae reached out to touch Eleret's head just above her eyebrow ridges. Then she reached for the special one. A healthy dragon of the same age would be a good comparison.

Rilli held still and proud as Jae felt her forehead, and then the small black dragon did the same.

Jae exhaled. No fever, unless dragons didn't show their fevers on their skin.

::We do.:: Two words from Kis that carried the weight of mountains.

She closed her eyes a moment, honoring his hard-won wisdom.

::Are there too many of us in your mind?:: Fendellen, speaking quietly.

Jae shook her head. She was glad to have them there, monitoring her thoughts, looking for something she might have missed.

::What is it you do now?:: Her dragon felt closer.

Jae looked down at her hands, surprised that they were moving. Her fingers stroked small circles on Eleret's chest, tracing the outlines of her scales. ::I'm not sure.:: It just felt right somehow. Calling the spirit of who the small dragon was to the surface.

::We can help with that.:: Fendellen's words were hushed. ::I can help with that.::

There would be questions later—but for now, it was enough to have the help. ::Slowly. We want to wake her very gently.::

::Perhaps the other two can move in closer?:: Her dragon's eyes swept over the two attentive hatchlings. ::She's used to waking up with them all nested together.::

It was a risk, but so was trying to wake Eleret—and so was letting her sleep. Healers rarely faced choices that came with guarantees of safety.

Jae wiggled her fingers at the two littles, motioning them in closer. They did so with speed and care and dignity, and it swelled her heart to watch them settle so very carefully around their fallen friend. Then she reached her mind for Fendellen—and jumped at what she felt there. More than just her dragon. Others, including some she knew.

::Dragons and kin. They all want to help.:: A moment of amusement from Fendellen. ::And Kellan, who somehow seems to be able to break all the rules.::

Jae didn't even know what those rules were, but she could feel the strength that had somehow joined Fendellen's end of the bond. Strength and steadiness. What to do with it was up to a healer and her dragon.

Jae gulped. She had been a healer before, and sometimes in dire circumstances, but this felt different. Bigger. There was no Gran who could be fetched by a quick runner. No wisdom story that would tell her how to wake a sleeping dragon.

Only her hands and her heart and what came to her through the bond.

She bowed her head and settled her hands, one on Eleret's belly, the other on her head. And began to sing. A song of the mountains, one that began as a lullaby and then grew fiercer. A song of the sun rising to meet the day in a part of the world where the days weren't always gentle and easy.

Eleret wiggled, and the two on each side of her snuggled in closer, their eyes wide, glued to the singing healer.

And to the call that came from the dragon at her shoulder. Jae could *feel* Fendellen's gentle tugging. A call with no words that spoke of bright skies and healthy wings and littles who had such courage that their bodies could barely contain it.

Jae let her song dance with what she could feel inside her. A call to body and spirit, and the reverent wishes of everyone inside the rondo and gathered outside it.

A small yellow head shot up, chittering, a black one right behind it.

Eleret's body tensed, a small being ready to hurtle herself into the sky—or astonished to discover she was no longer in it. Jae's hands firmed. It would not do for her patient to thrash. Not now.

Eleret's eyes opened, clearing as she looked at the two small faces jammed next to hers. Dimming with guilt as she surveyed the large circle gathered around her makeshift nest.

Jae kept her hands where they were. Sometimes, after danger, those who had been most scared got angry.

::Brave little healer.:: Kis stuck his nose into the hatchlings, but his words were for her. ::And not needed. No one would dare yell at Irin's babies.::

It was Irin she had been worried about.

::He's done all the yelling he has rights to in this lifetime.:: The big gold dragon nuzzled a tiny purple nose very carefully. ::We will talk to Eleret and make sure she understands the gravity of what she's done. But not today. Today is for being very glad she is still here to fuss over.::

Jae understood. These weren't only Irin's babies. They were Kis's, and Kellan's, and Inga's, and Fendellen's.

And now they were a little bit hers too.

CHAPTER 17

Fendellen tucked her tail under her nose and curled up against the wall. Carefully. The nursery was still very full of healing stuffs and extra food and four sleeping elves. Karis had brought blankets for Jae's friends, who had refused to leave as the young healer worked to restore Eleret to health.

It was good to see her kin so clearly finding her place in the village. Fendellen cast a fond gaze over the well-wrapped bundle sleeping next to the three dragonets. Jae's hand rested on Eleret's tail, and her wings sprawled over the nursery floor in the truest sign of her exhaustion.

Fendellen stoked the fire in her chest. It wasn't necessary—Kis kept the nursery warm with no need of any further help, even on the coldest nights. But she would do what little she could to add comfort to Jae's rest.

When she woke, Fendellen would need to say the words that would chase all that comfort away.

She flattened her head a little more onto her tail pillow.

Kis had said she would know, and he was right, but here in the quiet of a dark night and her own head, she could wish that her kin hadn't proven herself quite so worthy, at least not so soon. There was little doubt, however, that she had. Jae's healing skill had surprised even Irin, who had gracefully stepped back and let a human with wings serve in a role that had been his for as long as Fendellen could remember.

Healer might never have been one of his official titles, but it had always been one in fact. But the man who rarely deferred to anyone had calmly relegated himself to Jae's assistant. As had Inga and Kellan, Kis and Afran, and numerous others who never followed anyone who had not earned their respect.

Jae had led, and a dragon who would one day be queen could not ignore the significance of that any longer. Her kin might have come from a small mountain village, and she might have arrived overwhelmed and afraid, but necessity had called, and Jae had stepped up beautifully.

She deserved to know all of what called her.

The wings sprawled on the floor stirred, and Jae's head popped up. Her eyes cleared rapidly as she looked first at her patient, and then around the rondo.

Fendellen saw Kis and Irin both note her movement and then ease back into sleep. Warriors and healers, keeping the watch.

Jae, however, did not go back to sleep. Instead, she stretched out her arms and legs and very carefully unrolled herself from her blanket with the efficient stealth of one who had slept in tight quarters her whole life. She padded over to the table in her bare feet, picked up a cup of water, and crossed to Fendellen's side. ::Do you need anything?::

A small fraction of her kin's courage. Fendellen studied eyes that should have been glazed with exhaustion, but weren't. ::Sit with me for a while, sweet one. I would have the comfort of your presence.::

Jae gave her an odd look, but she took a seat on the soft straw and wrapped the wool blanket around her knees.

Fendellen wished for one of Kellan's berry tarts. A moment of tasty escape before she flung the two of them into realities far too hard. But it was midwinter, not the season for pastries that tasted of summer sun. ::There are things I must tell you. About who I am, and about who we are together.::

Jae didn't move, but Fendellen could feel her quickening attention through the bond. No fear, though. Not yet. Just nerves. And a fledging trust she was so very loath to weight this heavily.

::Is this about why you were the one who could call Eleret awake?::

Her kin did not lack for the ability to see clearly. ::Yes. Some dragons can feel those bonds to other dragons. Afran and Kis both can. It is part of why they are so respected.::

::And you.::

It wasn't a question. ::Yes. The strongest bonds live in our queens. Elhen. And one day, me.::

A long, silent pause in which Jae didn't so much as breathe. There was shock in the kin bond, and a slithering sense of unworthiness that Fendellen would have set on fire if she could. But there was very little surprise.

Finally, her kin sucked in a hitching breath. ::They follow you. I've seen it.::

If fire could not go after that unworthiness, perhaps words could. ::They follow you too. In the sky, and today as you healed one of our own.::

Denial, rising hot and swift—and on its heels, a healer's clear seeing. Commonsense clarity that would not allow Jae to ignore simple facts. She cuddled down into her feathers, a mess of dismay and confusion. ::I'm just an apprentice healer from a small mountain village.::

Fendellen nuzzled a shoulder clad in ice-blue wool. ::Apprentice healer and kin to a dragon queen.::

Jae's entire body shook. ::That isn't possible.::

Platitudes were too easy. Fendellen let her chin rest on Jae's shoulder. ::I feel that way some days too.::

The shaking eased as Jae's compassion rose taller than her fear. ::It's a really big job.::

The biggest. ::It's not mine yet. Mostly I get to fly around and cause trouble and keep everyone on their toes.::

Jae shook her head and rolled her eyes, snorting quietly into the dim. ::That's like Kis saying he mostly gets to lie around and eat all day.::

Fendellen winced at the well-landed arrow.

::He's a hero, even when he's eating stew.:: Slower words. More thoughtful ones. ::It's with him always. Just like being queen is always with you.::

::I will be queen after Elhen passes. Not yet.:: The distinction felt big and important.

Jae smiled. ::Apprentice queen, then.::

Fendellen had seen an apprentice step out of those

shoes today. She could only hope she would do so well when her turn came. ::Full healer and apprentice queen. We are a good pair.::

Jae shrugged. ::I would still be an apprentice in my village. It's only that you have no healer here. Although I think Irin is mostly one, and Kellan could be.::

Her kin had sharp eyes, and a heart that easily made space for others to step into all of who they were. Both very good qualities in one who was kin to a future queen. She had spent too much time looking at Jae's fears and not nearly enough time considering her strengths.

Jae looked over, and her eyes were gentle. Thoughtful. ::They all know, don't they.::

It wasn't a question, but Fendellen nodded anyway. ::I asked them to stay quiet. I wanted you to have a chance to find your place here first. To feel accepted for your hands and your wings and your heart.::

Jae cuddled her arms around her knees. ::Sometimes hiding is necessary.::

Perhaps. But always, it caused pain—and Fendellen hadn't considered that nearly enough either. ::I didn't trust your strength, and for that, I am sorry.::

Her kin blinked. ::Queens apologize?::

When they were wrong, which happened often enough. ::We are kin first.::

Fendellen paused as her own words landed. It felt right to say them, but they were a shocking violation of her most foundational promises. A queen's obligations came before everything. Before life. Before friends. Before self.

Royal responsibility—and royal isolation.

And yet, the star had given her a kin.

She felt her tail stirring, mirroring the unease inside her.

Jae reached out a hand, soothing, even in her own discomfort. ::Do you need anything? Food or water?::

::No. And if I did, I'm quite capable of fetching it myself.:: Fendellen knew she sounded cranky, but allowing others to serve her had always been one of the sorest points of her destiny.

An amused snort. ::I know that, but you're kind of big, and it's crowded in here, and if you knock something over and wake up the babies, Kis will have both our heads.::

Fendellen's eyes closed in bemused shame. Jae hadn't been trying to serve a dragon queen. She'd been trying to keep the two of them out of trouble.

A hand settled on her nose, warm and a little shaky. ::I think maybe you don't want me to treat you differently.::

Fendellen leaned into the tentative touch. ::An excellent diagnosis, young healer.::

Two arms, sneaking in to wrap around her neck. ::I can do that. I don't really know how to treat a queen anyhow. I will just treat you as my friend.::

One day, that would no longer be possible. One day, the promises running in her blood would need to take precedence. But for now, it suited an apprentice queen just fine. ::I would like that very much.::

Fendellen closed her eyes and sent a brief and heartfelt apology skyward.

One she hoped might be overheard by a star.

CHAPTER 18

*J*ae managed to peel her eyes open, although they felt like they had ended up under a snowbank overnight. The smells were worth it, though. Fresh bread, and warm cider, and the comforting whiff of oatmeal that said some things didn't change, no matter how far you wandered from home.

A big nose gently nudged her back and helped her sit up. ::Tired?::

She shouldn't be. Healers often went days without true sleep. Jae squinted. She'd gone to sleep by her patient, but she was waking up curled against her dragon. However, Eleret was clearly doing much better this morning, scrambling over to a bowl of milk curds with as much speed as her two nestling friends.

Irin, who was holding the bowl, looked over at Jae and nodded. A motion of both reassurance and dismissal. She wasn't needed.

She exhaled a long, slow sigh of relief. Young ones

mended very quickly once they got past the worst of things. Eleret was holding her wing gingerly, but she ate with relish, and anything too terribly painful would be putting her off her food.

They could apply more salve to her wing later—or let it ache a little, as a reminder of why hatchlings shouldn't undo window latches and fly out into unfriendly skies.

Jae was quite sure there would be new latches, and far more hatchling-proof ones, before sundown arrived. She stretched her arms over her head, working out the cricks that came from using a dragon as a pillow. Then she sensed Fendellen's careful attention behind her.

Jae turned, smiling at the ice-blue face that was becoming so familiar. ::What troubles you this morning?::

Her dragon's belly rumbled loudly.

All the heads in the rondo turned—and that's when Jae remembered. The conversation in the night. The one that had made everything make sense, all the strange looks and moments of everyday deference.

A rondo full of people who would be happy to fetch breakfast for a queen—and weren't sure if they should.

That was easily solved. Jae climbed to her feet. "Will you toast some cheese on bread for me?" Trift did that for Alonia, and it was delicious.

"No." Kis snorted from the corner. "There are only two dragons with permission to breathe fire in the village, and missy there is not one of them."

Jae hid a smile as her dragon offered up an exaggerated sulk. She remembered all of the conversation now, including the part where she'd promised to treat her dragon as a friend, not a queen. Clearly Kis kept a similar kind of promise, although his treatment of Fendellen tended a little more toward fondly annoyed guardian.

::She needs that too,:: said a deep voice in her head.

Jae swallowed as she gathered thick slices of bread and tasty cheese. Old warriors might be better at such steadiness.

Kellan held out her hands to take the sandwiches. "Fendellen can't toast them, but Kis might, if we ask him nicely." She fluttered her eyelashes at the old yellow dragon. "He has the finest aim in all the world."

Kis snorted. "You've been spending too much time with Alonia, I see."

Alonia was what Gran would have called a flirt—but the curvy blonde elf was also kindness personified. Jae held out two more sandwiches toward Kis. "They're my favorite, and I think there are three littles who could have a bite as well." She shot a look at three eager scaled faces. "A small bite." Curds weren't all that different from cheese, and they would enjoy the treat.

Irin handed her a pair of oversized metal forks. "Use these and hold a plate under the sandwiches or we'll have grease on the floor and hatchlings trying to lick the dirt."

A little dirt had never hurt anyone, but Jae had no intention of letting any yummy cheese drippings go to waste. She carefully threaded two sandwiches on each fork, and Kellan joined her with a fully loaded roasting fork in each hand as well. Apparently demand for toasted sandwiches was high. They held them out at arms' length, which was when Jae realized she was about to be on the business end of a blast of dragon fire.

Fendellen's laughter bubbled into her mind. ::Have no worries, sweet one. His aim is far better than mine.::

She didn't have any longer to worry as a stream of flame danced under the sandwiches and ended in a cast-iron skillet that Irin held out like he caught dragon fire every day of the week. Jae stared, and then caught herself as Karis and Sapphire hastily swung plates under the dripping cheese.

Laughter and more than one slightly burnt finger later, the sandwiches had been distributed, and Jae leaned back against her dragon. She broke her cheesy melted goodness in two and held out half.

::You eat it. Kellan has stew for me.::

Jae lifted her head and studied her dragon. There was more behind those words than generosity or an honest preference for stew.

A nose nuzzled her cheek. ::There is. I told you who I am last night. There is also something you need to know about who we are together. We'll go for a visit after you eat so that you can hear a story.::

Jae thought about that for a moment. There couldn't possibly be anything as life-altering as discovering the dragon who had rescued you from freezing to death was apprentice dragon royalty. And she liked stories. She took a big bite of her sandwich, which was absolutely delicious —and almost cool enough not to burn her tongue. "All right. Who are we going to visit?"

Silence landed in the rondo, and Jae realized she'd spoken out loud. She swallowed quickly, and turned. Everyone watched the two of them, even the babies, who couldn't possibly know why everyone was staring. Or maybe they did. Jae realized she knew very little about what it meant to be a dragon queen.

"Good." Kis's rumble was audible, and approving. "You told her."

"I told her I will be queen." Fendellen's tone was one Jae had never heard. Commanding. Regal. "It is for Elhen to tell her the rest."

Jae spun around again, her head dizzy. "We're going to visit the dragon queen? Now?"

Fendellen snorted, amused. "Yes. In her cave. But eat your sandwich first, or she'll finish it for you. She's rather fond of toasted cheese."

Jae blinked. And swallowed. She might be able to treat one dragon queen as a friend. She was absolutely certain that number didn't extend to two.

CHAPTER 19

*J*ae could feel her legs trying to turn to water. Somewhere on the way up to the cave, they had realized she was on her way to see royalty. Real royalty, not the friendly apprentice kind. There was a world of difference between Mellie and Gran, and just as much between Fendellen and the old and powerful dragon she had met briefly on the cliffs.

She stepped into the cave, holding tight to a wrapped packet of bread and cheese. The toasting forks were in her pocket. Apparently Fendellen hadn't exaggerated the queen's fondness for the tasty snack.

Two dragons greeted them, shoulder to shoulder, and then separated on some unseen command to create a narrow entry into the cave.

Fendellen bowed her head, first right and then left. "Ciara. Jarden."

Dragons guarding the gates. Jae gulped. Someone very important lived inside. Fendellen nudged her back, none too gently, and she made her way between the two dragons. She didn't gulp when she arrived in the cavern proper. She couldn't. She was too busy gaping at all the shiny treasures. There were goblets and shiny rocks and paintings and fabrics in colors her fingers itched to touch.

"Elhen." Fendellen's voice was quiet, but easily heard in the cave. "We greet you."

"Welcome." The queen's reply was warm and inviting. "Do come in." She looked straight at Jae. "I've had them bring some pillows and a blanket for you, youngling, but please speak up if you're cold."

The cave was as warm as the nursery. "I'm fine, thank you." Jae tried not to gape at the beautiful things everywhere her eye could see. She yanked her eyes back to the queen. "I'm very sorry. There's just so much to look at."

Elhen inclined her head regally. "It is never wrong to appreciate a dragon's treasure. You are welcome to look more closely after I have told you of the prophecy."

Jae blinked. She had come to hear a story. Prophecy sounded far scarier. Her belly tightened, and she began to regret the second cheese sandwich.

She let Fendellen's nose push her over to a small pile of pillows in beautiful, rich colors. On any other day, she would have been enchanted. On this one, she just felt small and scared.

The queen studied her intently as Fendellen settled at her side. "I shall begin so that you do not let fear drain you any further."

Jae winced. She'd hoped her feelings weren't quite so obvious.

"These are the words that have been told, passed down

from queen to queen, beginning with Lovissa, the great warrior dragon. She is the grandmother of my grandmother, twenty-five generations past. This is the story that has been passed from Lovissa to me."

Jae recognized a skilled storyteller when she heard one. Elhen would have been welcomed in any hamlet in the mountains. In human form, anyhow. She winced again and focused on the words of the old queen. The one whose scales somehow shone as bright as treasure even in the dim light of the cave.

Her words, however, were not shiny. They spoke of battles, fierce and gruesome, and dragonkind at the very brink, of dragonkiller arrows and scaled warriors lost forever to magics and treachery.

She gulped. Her own ears weren't pointed, but she counted elves amongst her new friends.

::As do we, sweet one.:: Fendellen's whisper soothed her some, but it couldn't take away the anguish of imagining so many dragons dead.

Elhen paused, studying her with eyes that had seen both far and deep for longer than Jae could imagine. "It did not end the way the dragons of old feared," the queen said quietly. "We do not know the full story of how they were saved, for that has been lost in the fires of time. But the wisdom of the queens has passed on this much."

Jae felt the old dragon's power gathering.

"There will be five," Elhen intoned. "Five dragons and their kin who will come to save the dragons of old. They will be marked by the Dragon Star, who will place a light just above their eyes."

She turned the full force of her gaze on Jae. "It is a mark that will be visible only to the eyes of a queen."

Jae felt her insides turn to springmelt—and then to vapor.

She felt her dragon stir beside her.

Elhen's chastening gaze turned to Fendellen. "Respect her strength. She grows in knowledge and she arrived wise, and she has strength that even you don't understand yet. Do not shield her when it is not necessary."

Fendellen's movements ceased.

Jae tried to meet the queen's eyes. She cleared her throat, and then cleared it again when no words came out. "Am I marked?" She turned to her dragon and stared at Fendellen's forehead. "Is she?"

"Yes." A single word that reverberated through the entire cave.

"What does that even mean?"

It took Jae a moment to realize the harsh whisper had been hers.

::We don't know,:: Fendellen said gently. ::We know only that we will be called, and we must do our very best to be ready.::

It felt like the night of snowstorms and demon dragons again. Entirely unreal.

"It's very real." Elhen spoke briskly. "You are the fourth pair to be marked."

There were others. Somehow that gave Jae's chest just enough space to breathe.

The queen's crisp nod reminded her of Gran. "You know them. Sapphire and Lotus were first, and if you feel ill equipped for this job, imagine young Sapphire, sitting high in a tree with a screeching hatchling in her lap."

Jae had heard that story. Apparently with rather a large omission.

"Your kin asked that you not be told until she deemed you ready."

Elhen's words held no opinion, no censure, but Jae heard some anyhow. That straightened her spine. "I thought her a demon when we first met. I wouldn't have believed this."

Something in the queen's eyes softened. "Your loyalty is noted, youngling."

Jae swallowed. "There are others?"

"Lily and Oceana." Fendellen sounded amused. "Lily had to wade through a swamp to get to her dragon. I should perhaps not have been surprised to find you in foul weather."

Two who were her friends. Jae felt her chest growing tight again.

"Three." Fendellen's nose settled against her shoulder. "Alonia and Trift as well."

The kind elf and her laughing dragon. Something caught in Jae's heart. Three of her friends—and not the fourth. She turned to the old queen, the question spurting out before she could catch its tail. "Not Kellan?"

A long pause, one that seemed somehow full of aching. "Young Kellan has not been marked."

That wasn't fair. Jae had been in the village only a few days and she already knew Kellan was the very best of them.

"We don't know how the Dragon Star chooses, or why."

Elhen was back to sounding regal. "We know only that it does."

Jae felt her head swirling like the winds caught in a tight valley. She had been chosen for a task so huge, it might as well be moving mountains with a spoon. Her. A girl from a remote village with wings and some small healing skill.

And a dragon queen as her kin.

Jae gulped. The star had chosen Fendellen. She was just a small weed plucked up along with a useful plant.

::I am not at all sure of that,:: said a quietly regal voice inside her head. The queen gave Fendellen a look that brooked no disobedience. "I would talk to your kin for a moment alone. You may go outside on the cliffs and help Ciara toast my cheese sandwiches."

Jae tried to straighten because as fierce as that look was, she wasn't sure her dragon would go unless her kin looked a lot less like a leaf about to blow off a tree. She set back her shoulders and spread her wings a little to show the tiny beads she hadn't been able to work up the will to take off.

Elhen glanced at her, and Jae was quite sure she saw approval in the old, dark eyes.

"Go," said the queen to the dragon hovering at her shoulder. "She will do you proud, this day and many others. And I'm far too old to eat a human without getting terrible indigestion."

Whatever had made Jae's spine stiffen promptly melted.

But it was too late. Fendellen had already left the cave.

*T*he queen studied Jae again. ::I'm sorry, youngling. You would think that at my age, I would have learned not to make inappropriate jokes. Dragons have not eaten humans in my lifetime, or in those of any of my grandmothers of memory. The tales sometimes say otherwise, but those are the ramblings of humans who would rather believe in evil dragons than in far more ordinary dangers.::

Jae swallowed hard. There were plenty of ordinary dangers in the high mountains.

::There are. You have grown up used to risk. I believe that will serve you well.::

It was good to know she had some small skills that might be useful. ::If the star wanted a healer, it would have been far smarter to pick my gran.::

::The star has not picked our obviously best and brightest.:: The queen paused. ::And yet over time, I have begun to have more faith in its choices.::

Jae wasn't at all sure she agreed, but her bones were too soft to argue with a queen and a star both.

::Stories need time to settle, and you will take yours.:: Elhen regarded her silently for a moment. ::I kept you here to offer you two things. One is a gift. The other is a word of advice about that dragon of yours.::

Jae sat up straighter. There was an odd sharpness in the queen's words.

::It is not sharpness,:: the queen said quietly. ::It is fear, and perhaps regret. Do you know what it is that Fendellen fears most deeply?::

Jae opened her mouth and then closed it again. She

took her time, making a tea with all the bits and pieces she had gathered since the night a demon dragon had plucked her out of a storm. ::She fears to be alone.::

::Yes.:: Clear, proud eyes—and ineffable sadness. ::She fears to be like me.::

Jae gaped.

::The walk of a queen is a challenging one. I have chosen to do it alone, separated, as did the one who was queen before me.::

Jae dug out one of the bits she had tucked away. ::Kis is your friend.::

Surprise—and fondness. ::Kis is dear to me. But I have never let him be as close as he would wish to be. I told myself the distance was necessary, that it made me a better queen.:: A long exhale. ::Perhaps it has.::

It was hard not to turn away from the pressing sadness. Jae reached into it instead. ::Gran says the same about being a healer. Your heart can't get too close or your mind won't have the space it needs to think clearly.::

More surprise. Warmth. ::Ah, you understand then.:: A pause, one so long Jae thought the words might be done. ::And you perhaps understand some of the cost.::

Jae's heart squeezed. ::You did not choose a kin?::

A regal head, slowly shaken. ::No. Or perhaps I did not let one choose me.::

Jae straightened her shoulders. ::Fendellen isn't alone. I won't let her be.::

The pride in the queen's eyes was unmistakable. ::She will need that fierceness from you, youngling. Even now, she holds back the last of her loneliness from you.::

Jae's hands formed into fists. "That's not true."

A sigh. "It is true, but my words were perhaps clumsy. She accepts your bond fully now. But she believes that one day, she will need to step into loneliness again."

Jae didn't understand—and then she did. "When she becomes queen."

A long, slow nod. "Yes. She would protect you still."

Fire rose from Jae's belly, traveling up to wrap around her chest. Her throat. ::She can try.::

Rumbling laughter from the queen, and flashing, fierce pleasure. ::Oh, she has chosen well. Does she know what a temper you have when you're finally lit?::

Jae grinned. ::Not yet.::

::Ah, I would see that day.:: The queen nodded her head sharply. ::Come. I have a small gift for you, and your dragon grows restless.::

Jae could feel that through their bond. She sent soothing. Calming. The kin version of chamomile tea.

The queen walked a few steps and stopped, her chin pointing at a small box on a table with no other treasure. ::Open it. What is inside is for you.::

Jae walked over with no small trepidation.

"There are beads in your wings. They are very pretty." Elhen nodded her head toward the small box. "Perhaps you would add a few more to their number."

Gingerly, Jae lifted the lid off the exquisitely crafted box —and gaped at what she saw inside. Gorgeous, glimmering flakes of ice, catching the dim light in the cave and turning it into stars.

She reached out a shaking finger, knowing full well they weren't really flakes of ice, or stars, or simple beads. They were something she had seen only rarely in the high mountains, and only in a family's most treasured possessions.

Jewels.

She gulped. She couldn't possibly take them, but she had no idea how to turn down the gift of a queen.

"All dragons have some fondness for treasure." Elhen sounded like she was describing a particularly tasty bit of cheese. "I have caves full, and rarely do I have a chance to give any of my pretties to someone who will properly appreciate them."

Pretty was entirely the wrong word. They were dazzling. Breathtaking.

"They are a suitable gift for the one who will wear them."

Jae heard the message behind the words. These weren't for her, healer girl from the high mountains. They were for the kin of one who would be queen.

::They are for both. Don't forget your girl from the mountains, youngling.:: The queen's voice was stern, and it resonated somewhere deep in Jae's head. ::That is who the star chose, and I believe that is who Fendellen needs.::

Jae stared at the jewels as the words seeped into the new tea she had already begun. This one was so very important. She could feel that in every bit of the healer Gran had painstakingly trained. A monumental tea. One that would touch souls.

She smiled at the jewels. She knew exactly what she needed to add next.

CHAPTER 20

"They're so shiny." Alonia talked around the pins in her mouth.

"They look like raindrops froze in your feathers." Kellan carefully stitched another of Elhen's jewels onto Jae's wings, each one added individually so no threads would hamper her flight. It was delicate, time-consuming work—and her friends had jumped at the chance to spend their day adorning her wings.

Lily and Sapphire had tried to volunteer too, but Alonia had overruled them, claiming they would manage to sew Jae's sleeves to her wings or some other calamity. So those two were quietly taking care of some other things that needed to happen this day instead. Things a healer having jewels stitched to her wings didn't have time to do.

Kellan smoothed another of the jewel beads into place and smiled. "Are your wings tired yet? Do you need a break?"

They'd been holding up their arms for as long as she'd

been holding up her wings. "I could go ask Inga nicely for some lunch."

"We already did." Sapphire danced in the door with a tray and grinned at the elf behind her. "Well, *I* asked nicely. Lily stood in the corner and scowled, so she probably got the moldy loaf of bread."

Jae was quite sure Inga would never allow such a thing in her kitchen. She smiled at the newcomers. "That smells delicious."

"Not as delicious as what else she's cooking." Sapphire set down the tray, her eyes glinting in conspiratorial happiness. "Karis had some special spices, and Irin went hunting, and Ana went to the village down the road and came back with all the butter they could spare. There will be so many meat pies. Fendellen will be so surprised."

Jae could feel her heart swelling. She had hoped people would help without asking too many questions, but this was more than she could have imagined. Even her four closest friends didn't know all of what she planned, although perhaps they had some guesses.

Kellan picked up a slice of bread and buttered it thickly. Then she handed it to Jae, who was still waiting for Alonia to finish sewing on a jewel. "Are the villagers talking?"

"Of course." Lily rested her knees against a bedpost and nibbled on a square of cheese. "They're all a-dither about four being marked now."

Four sets of eyes turned her way.

Lily snorted. She raised an eyebrow at Kellan. "Some are saying you'll be the fifth."

That was just like Lily. Brutally direct and kind, all at

the same time. Saying what might otherwise be said in whispers.

Kellan shrugged. "They've been saying the next dragon would be mine for a long time too. So far, they've been wrong."

Elhen was right. Courage came in many different forms. Jae reached out for the food tray and added two spoonfuls of jam on top of her bread and butter. Then she handed it to the small elf who waited and somehow chose to be useful and cheerful instead of bitter and sad.

Kellan smiled and bit into the extra helping of jam.

Jae slid down the wall next to her. Trying, with all the small, everyday motions of friendship to include the one who could feel so very excluded. She had spent her whole life on the receiving end of those small barbs. "The villagers are just hoping the star doesn't decide to pick one of them. From what I can tell, being marked just leaves you wet and cold or with a sore head."

Alonia giggled. "Or bruised ribs."

Jae winced. She hadn't been to weapons training yet, and she was not looking forward to it. "I should have made more salve."

"That salve is really helping Kis." Lily shot Jae a look. "I heard Irin tell Karis that he slept as easily last night as he does in the summer. Usually the winters are really hard for him."

That warmed Jae right from the depths of her belly. "I don't know if there's enough to last until spring." She'd made as big a batch as she dared with the ingredients she had, but Gran hadn't expected her to be dosing dragons. "I might try to fly back in the first spring melts." It would be dangerous, and cold, but worth it.

Lily snorted. "Do that alone and your dragon will disown you. Or issue a royal edict or something."

Jae rolled her eyes. In very short order, her four friends had turned the idea of being kin to a dragon queen into a standing joke. Which was far better than the alternative, so she wasn't going to issue a word of complaint, other than the obviously expected ones. "What can she do, deprive me of bread and toasted cheese?"

"Probably." Kellan grinned. "Inga really likes Fendellen."

That would be why the cook was currently making dozens of meat pies instead of the small plate of them Jae had very tentatively requested. Her dragon might be important, but it seemed more significant to Jae that she was loved.

That was the true gift of this place.

She took a bite of her bread and butter, suddenly shaky. She had planned this day for her dragon, but also for herself. She wanted to soak in the best parts of what it meant to be kin, to belong, to have friends who chattered away as they sewed jewels from a dragon queen to her feathers, and then sat on the floor and ate bread and jam and cheese together like it was just a normal day.

It was a gift to a human girl born with wings, and, she hoped, to a dragon who had been born to be queen—and was somehow convinced she would need to walk her life's path alone. Jae knew what it was to believe that so deeply it was etched on her very bones. She'd grown up watching the others of the village form friendships and have babies and laugh and cry together for big reasons and small ones, and believed it was her lot to always walk on the edges of that. To watch, and to be tolerated, even appreciated, but never quite included.

She knew what such believing did to the shape of a heart.

Today, she wanted to set Fendellen's heart free to be the shape it needed to be.

She took in another shaky breath and took a big bite of her bread. Healers knew that hunger and thirst could undo a proper healing, and whatever else this afternoon might be, it was a healing of sorts. She wouldn't go into it with an empty belly.

Kellan's hand settled gently on her arm. No words. No questions. Just presence.

Jae offered the small elf a smile. Then she looked around the room. At Alonia, one cheek full as a chipmunk's, carefully threading needles for the last few jewels. At Sapphire, tossing bread out the window Lily had opened and laughing as a large pink tongue caught the tossed snack. At Lily, shaking her head and offering the last of her bread for dragon feeding.

All of them acknowledging the invisible marks on their foreheads—or the lack of one—and holding tight to steadfastly ordinary lives anyhow. And they had somehow included her in their number.

They were five. Perhaps not the five of prophecy, or the five the star would finally pick for whatever destiny lay ahead, but they were five nonetheless. Five in friendship, in strength, in honest acceptance of each other, the weaknesses and the strengths.

She let it wash over her. Let herself lean into it and grow strong from it. Let it steep inside her because this was the most important ingredient of the tea she was making, and the one with which she was least familiar. She tried not to let that worry her overmuch. Healers sometimes had to use new medicines, especially when they proved so very well suited to the task.

She let out a breath and shook her head. So very presumptuous, she was, believing she could heal one who would be queen. But she could feel the voice inside her. The tugging. The same insanity that had called her out on a dark night and away from her home and into near death.

She swallowed hard. Elhen believed she was worthy to be Fendellen's kin. So did the four friends making short work of bread and cheese and jewels.

Even a star believed.

Now all that was necessary was that a human girl left to die in the high mountains might spread her newly jeweled wings and believe it too.

CHAPTER 21

*J*ae looked over at the mouth of the cave. The old and nearly translucent queen dropped her chin ever so slightly in acknowledgment, perhaps even in support. But Jae knew the truth. She stood on this cliff alone.

She held out her wings, letting the bright noonday sun catch the jewels and make them radiant.

Heads snapped to attention. Dozens of them, dragons and villagers both, standing on boulders and craning for a better view.

Jae lifted into the air so they could have it. So many had come, even the large and pained yellow dragon and his three miraculously well-behaved charges. Inga was there, with bread flour still on her skirts, and Ana had brought a wagon for the children to stand on so they could see. Irin stood proudly at Kis's shoulder, and Karis perched on Afran's head, two sets of wise eyes studying her with calm curiosity.

Every one of them here simply because she had invited them. To a ceremony with no name and a ritual she was about to make up out of thin air. Which was right and proper. As any flier knew, it was the thinnest air, the highest air—the air that had kissed high mountains—that held the most power.

And the most risk.

She couldn't let that shake her now. Jae ran her hands down the ice-blue tunic and its silver stitching. She was about to issue an edict to a queen, and that wasn't going to work if she quivered while she said the words. She raised her head and called for the dragon that couldn't possibly have missed the gathering of every living being in the village. "Fendellen. Dragon who chose me. I call you to join me."

The words rang out over those gathered, and somehow, in the crisp, cold light, they didn't sound nearly as silly as when she'd imagined them in her own head.

For a long moment, nothing—and then Afran's head turned.

The incoming ice-blue streak circled the gathered crowd, at a distance and speed that nearly blurred her. Jae pivoted in the sky, always facing her dragon.

Fendellen circled closer on a long, majestic glide. Then she pointed her nose into the sky, a sharp, zooming climb —and at the top, a twist into a spectacular, glistening dive that captured the streaming sunlight on her wings.

Jae grinned. Her dragon certainly knew how to make an entrance. That was good. At least one of them should.

::This is not too shabby for your first effort,:: came the wry reply.

Something that had been tight in Jae's chest all day relaxed. The bond was there, full and bright and resonant, and nothing she could do or say in the next moments would shake that. She held up her arms to the dragon above her in the sky.

Fendellen tucked in her wings and shot downward, a hurtling ball of dragon headed straight for Jae's outstretched fingers.

She didn't move a muscle.

A collective hiss from the crowd, and then Fendellen tucked and rolled, zooming out so close to the ground that even Jae's breath caught, and buzzing by the crowd close enough to shake whiskers and scales.

Eleret got waist-high into the sky before Irin nabbed her.

Jae grinned. Every ritual needed a noisy toddler or two.

Fendellen swept by the last of the gathered crowd and angled toward Jae. More slowly now, with grace and strength and dawning majesty.

Jae hovered in the sky and waited for her queen.

::Not yet.:: Fendellen came to a stop, face to face and heart to heart, so close their wing tips skimmed the same air. ::I am not your queen yet.::

Jae raised her hands to each side of an ice-blue nose. She paused and took in a breath.

The tea was ready.

"I thought you were a demon." Jae pitched her voice in the way of the people of the high mountains when they needed to be heard. "You came to me on a fierce winter night. I saw your face in the ice and snow and thought you were my death."

"I thought you were dead." Fendellen's voice rang clear and crisp and true. A dragon who might not know why she had been called, but knew how to tell a good story anyway.

The silence below them was absolute. Even the littles stared up in awe.

"I woke up in warmth, in a cave with a pool of warm water and a dragon who matched the color of the moonlight."

Fendellen's eyes glinted with humor. "You called me demon, even as your teeth chattered."

Jae wasn't entirely sure if that was true, but she had surely thought it. "I come from the high mountains, where the winters take many lives. Where the people are good, and hard working, and kind, but not always so trusting of those who are different." She steadied her voice. "On my way here, I discovered the people of the lowlands are sometimes like that too."

She could feel Fendellen's pain through their bond. Her sorrow. A queen who felt guilt for not protecting one she hadn't even known yet.

That needed to stop. "I was left on the side of a mountain to die, and found kindness instead. I grew up knowing love, and I grew up knowing what it was to be different, always. I learned to heal, and I learned to persist because the high mountains rarely forgive those who quit." She angled her wings to catch the sun. "I learned to fly like the eagles. My wings were my biggest fear and my greatest solace."

She breathed out. It ran contrary to everything Gran had ever taught her to talk so much about herself, but the details mattered. "This was my journey, and I believe it was for a reason."

Fendellen's cheek leaned into her hand. "It made you a kin fit for a queen."

That was almost right. "It made me a kin fit for *one* queen."

The ice-blue dragon stared.

"I am *your* kin. I am not meant to be royalty. I'm here to be your friend. To say, in front of all these witnesses, that you will never walk alone." Jae dropped the most bitter herb into the tea. "Even when you are queen."

Fendellen froze.

Speaking about her dragon's most private pain was even more counter to everything Jae knew—but it was also necessary. Some pains had to be seen to be properly lanced. "You believe that is a thing you will do alone."

A long, fierce silence in which Jae understood just what it was to have stirred the fire of a dragon. "So it has always been."

She wasn't going to argue dragon history with a dragon. She would leave that to Elhen, or to Fendellen's own fearsome honesty. "I hear dragons have never tumbled-rolled in the sky, either."

A surprised, and amused, snort that nearly singed her eyebrows.

Jae smiled. "You aren't a dragon bound by rules."

::Do you know what it is that you do, sweet one?:: A wry question, and a pointed one.

Not any more than when she had flown off into the bitter-cold dark, following the voice of a star. But this felt just as important. ::I fight so that neither of us are lonely ever again.::

Fendellen hissed—and all the anger inside her died.

A warm blue nose touched her cheek, light as a feather. ::I wish that it were possible.:: Sadness poured through the bond. ::You don't understand, sweet one. It isn't the queen who chooses the distance. It is those she rules.::

It took every bit of strength Jae had to push away. She spread her wings again, letting the jewels of an old and perhaps regretful queen shine light into the dark. "I can't speak for those of the past. I can't even speak for those of now, except for me. But I can guess."

She looked down at the gathered crowd. "Kis treats you as a hatchling still, and you allow it. Lotus won't remember to treat you like a queen for any longer than her next barrel roll. Afran might try to respect you from a distance, but the woman sitting on his head will likely have a thing or two to say about that."

Karis waved cheerfully.

Jae turned to face her dragon, but she could feel the air currents of support from those gathered below. "I came here as one who had always been held at a distance because of my wings. Not a single person or dragon here ever backed away from me because of them, but I couldn't see that. Not until you made me look."

Fendellen blinked.

Jae smiled. "You sent me friends to decorate my wings, and cooks bearing brooms to make me feel useful, and old dragons to help me see wisdom."

Laughter rang below them, loud and clear.

The ice-blue dragon cast Kis a wry look. "He did his part all by himself."

Jae grinned. She had guessed mostly right.

Now for the wildest guess of all. She sobered and stretched out her wings and arms, doing her very best to look regal. "We are marked of the Dragon Star. I don't know why, and I don't know what we will be called to do. But I see your strength, Fendellen who will be queen. I see your heart, and I saw you set fire to the distance I wrapped around myself like a warm winter cloak." She gulped. "I won't let you wear that cloak either."

Fendellen bowed her head. A dragon acknowledging the only royal command Jae ever intended to make. She closed the small distance between them in the sky and hugged her dragon long and tight and hard.

Saw, out of the corner of her eye, the regal nod of an old queen.

Heard the loud cheering of the crowd below—and then their hushed awe.

Slowly, Jae and her dragon lifted their heads, staring. Green lights and blue ones, yellows and flares of pink danced around them, painting the entire sky.

The breath of the Dragon Star.

EPILOGUE

*L*ovissa woke from her dream, jerked awake by a call to battle.

She reached the mouth of her cave before she realized there was no movement in the valley below. No bugling, no dragon trumpeting his alert to the skies. Only silence.

She reached out with the power of a queen, yanking her finest warrior and the leader of her scouts out of sleep. ::There is danger.::

::Where?:: A single word, from a dragon she could already see winging into the skies.

She did not know. ::Look everywhere.::

More fliers in the sky, soundless, that they might not alert the enemy to their awakening. Forms, little more than shadow, heading north and south. Searching for the invading hordes.

She stood at attention, old and useless, and waited for their reports. She did not know what had awakened her, but it had a fierce hold on her still. The looming wings of destiny.

Her breath caught. So might a queen feel at the moment of her death.

She turned to face the Dragon Star, choking back her fire with only the greatest of effort. ::Not today. It must not be today. Quira is so very tiny yet. Do not doom my dragons so.::

A black shape landed beside her in the night. ::It is not the elves. There is no sign of them, and the snow in the passes is still impenetrable.::

Battles had been lost when leaders had been wrong about such things.

::It is not the elves. They could not move around on such a night without been seen. Nor set fires to keep warm while they slept.::

Her heart still beat wildly in her chest, but the rest of her was beginning to listen to reason. ::I was yanked from my sleep, Baraken. I know not why. But the blood of all the queens that have come before lives in me, and it stirs violently this night.

Something comes for us.:: She resisted the last words, but he needed to hear them. ::Or for me.::

Alarm—and then a long, steady assessment. ::You look in fine form.::

She felt in fine form, other than the panic trying to take wing deep inside her. ::Then something else.:: Something with the kind of urgency she had never felt in her lifetime.

And then she looked up at the Dragon Star, and she knew.

Lovissa let the knowing sink into her blood and find confirmation there because she had already sent alarm ringing through her dragons without thinking first, and she was deeply embarrassed to have done it once, let alone twice.

Baraken stood, a silent sentinel at her side.

She bowed her head, the weight of what she found in her

blood so very heavy that even a queen could hardly bear it. She shook herself and tried to deny. To resist. It made no sense. There were only four. The prophecy spoke of five. They had time yet.

The star's implacable message did not change.

It was time.

THANK YOU

As you might have guessed, there is one final Dragon Kin book still coming. To hear about the final release, head to audreyfayewrites.com and sign up for the *New Releases* email list.

If you're a reader who likes to graze widely, you might enjoy some of Audrey's other books while you wait. There's everything from spacefaring singers to assassins and mermaids.

Happy reading,
Shae & Audrey

Made in the USA
San Bernardino, CA
03 March 2019